Amy's Dream Proposal:

1. Groom-to-be on bended knee—after all, only successful proposals are made in person.

2. Big bouquet of flowers—hope I'm not allergic!

3. Moonlight serenade—no tone-deaf musicians, please.

4. The biggest "rock" he can afford—after all, they'll all be comparing at the office.

5. Make sure he's absolutely, positively in love with me (and it's not just the champagne talking)!

Dear Reader,

Romance in the workplace. Everyone says it shouldn't happen—and everyone knows it happens anyway. I currently work in an office full of women—no hope of romance there. But I remember one summer when I was cashiering at the local grocery store to earn extra money for college—and to pay for my horse. The manager was one of those good-looking flirts with a smile to die for. Unfortunately, he flirted with everyone and went further with no one. But I do remember how flattered I was when my parents came up to school to visit me and he'd sent along a bouquet. (Of daisies, mind you, but flowers all the same.) Anyway, Jeannie Renamo, heroine of Lynda Simons' *Marrying Well*, has a lot better luck with her boss. Kyle Hunter is, quite simply, the perfect man for her—something they're both about to find out.

And then there's Toni Collins' newest, *The Almost-Perfect Proposal*. It takes a fifty-year-old proposal gone astray to introduce Amy Barrington to Brian Reynolds, but it's clearly not going to take Brian another fifty years to utter a proposal of his own. Sometimes it's a good thing the mail isn't always reliable!

Enjoy both these wonderful books, and rejoin us next month here at Yours Truly, because we'll be bringing you two more books about unexpectedly meeting, dating—and marrying!—Mr. Right.

Leslie Wainger,
Senior Editor and Editorial Coordinator

Please address questions and book requests to:
Silhouette Reader Service
U.S.: 3010 Walden Ave., P.O. Box 1325, Buffalo, NY 14269
Canadian: P.O. Box 609, Fort Erie, Ont. L2A 5X3

TONI COLLINS

The Almost-Perfect Proposal

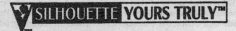

SILHOUETTE YOURS TRULY™

Published by Silhouette Books
America's Publisher of Contemporary Romance

For Dawn Cresswell and Pearl Wilson, with love

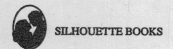 SILHOUETTE BOOKS

ISBN 0-373-52041-7

THE ALMOST-PERFECT PROPOSAL

This edition published by arrangement with Harlequin Books S.A.

® and TM are trademarks of Harlequin Books S.A., used under license.
Trademarks indicated with ® are registered in the United States Patent
and Trademark Office, the Canadian Trade Marks Office and in other
countries.

Printed in U.S.A.

About the author

"I can't remember a time when I didn't want to be a novelist. As early as the third grade, I can recall being hauled off to the principal's office because I was caught writing short stories in class. The best grade I ever got in high school was for a short story about wacky time travelers written as a special project in history class. I wrote my first novel when I was seventeen, but it took me another eighteen years to get published. Perseverance pays!

"I was born and raised in St. Louis, where I still live with my teenage son, who stopped calling me 'Mom' when he was six, and my mom (I still call her 'Mom' because I want to go on living!)."

The Almost-Perfect Proposal is Toni Collins's ninth novel for Silhouette Books.

Books by Toni Collins

Silhouette Yours Truly

*Un*Happily *Un*Wed
The Almost-Perfect Proposal

Silhouette Desire

Immoral Support #686

Silhouette Romance

Ms. Maxwell and Son #664
Letters from Home #893
Something Old #941
Miracle Dad #1008
Miss Scrooge #1050
Willfully Wed #1159

1

Boston

"This is a joke, right?" Amy Barrington asked.

Shaking his head, the mailman looked apologetic. "'Fraid not," he said, handing her the envelope. "I don't know why it took so long to get here—but better late than never, I suppose."

Amy took it from him. "I'd say that depends on what's inside," she responded warily. "Thanks, Harry."

"Hope it's not bad news."

"That makes two of us."

Amy closed the front door. She stared at the envelope, still unable to believe it. This letter had been lost in the mail for more than fifty years. The letter, postmarked July 2, 1944, had been mailed from Europe during World War II, and it was addressed to her mother!

Do I open it, she wondered, glancing up the staircase. *Or just give it to her?*

Do I dare take that chance?

It could be risky, she told herself as she made her way up the stairs. Her mother was in poor health—and whatever the contents of this letter, it was bound to have a profound impact on the elderly woman.

Amy was going to have to give this some serious thought.

Passing her mother's closed door, she took the letter to her room. The name on the return address was one she couldn't help but recognize: John Reynolds. He was the man her mother had mentioned many times these past eight months that Amy had lived with her.

John Reynolds had been the one great love of Marian Haskell's life.

If only he hadn't gone off to war, Amy thought, they might have gotten married.

Amy had dearly loved her father, and she knew that Marian and Charles Barrington had been totally devoted to each other in their forty years of marriage. But being a die-hard romantic, Amy couldn't help but wonder what might have been. What did true love feel like? Was it falling in love in such a romantic way, through the mail across thousands of miles and an ocean the way her mother had with John Reynolds? Amy had always been enchanted by the stories her mother had told her, by John's letters, so full of danger and excitement. She remembered one in particular, about a mission that took him to Paris. He wrote of seeing couples at the sidewalk cafés and thinking of Marian and how he'd like to take her there someday. There was a war going on, and each day could have been his last, but his thoughts were still always for her.

That, Amy told herself, was love.

Fingering the tattered edges of the envelope in her hand, she wished she knew....

The letter her mother received from John Reynolds had made Amy stop and think about her own love life.

Or more appropriately, her lack of one.

If only she could forget the pain her ex-husband had caused her....

"Where are you going?" Amy asked, looking up from the paperwork on her desk.

Parker stood in the doorway to her office. "I'm leaving. Moving out."

Her husband's tone was unbearably cold. "I want a divorce, Amy."

Until that moment, Amy hadn't had a clue that there had been anything at all wrong in her marriage. She'd met her husband, Parker Ryan, in college. She was a liberal arts major; he was working on his M.B.A. They'd known each other almost four years before getting married, and Amy thought she'd known all there was to know about him going into the marriage.

Apparently she'd been wrong.

"I don't understand..." Amy began.

"What's not to understand?" he asked. "I want a divorce. That's pretty simple."

"But why? We haven't been having any problems."

"We haven't had much of anything lately," he snapped. "You've had your life and I've had mine. We've grown apart, Amy. You can't deny that."

"I—I suppose we haven't spent much time together lately," she admitted.

"You've been spending more time with Adam McCabe than you have with me," he reminded her.

"That's not fair, Parker. It's professional! I don't like it any more than you do," she insisted. "In fact, I probably like it even *less* than you do."

"I don't like it or dislike it," he maintained. "It's not my problem anymore."

It didn't make any sense to Amy. Parker couldn't possibly be jealous of a man who didn't even exist. Adam McCabe was fictional.

Seven years ago she'd written and sold her first mystery novel. Unfortunately, her publishers didn't think a hard-boiled detective character created by a woman would sell, so they'd insisted she use a male pseudonym. She'd hated the idea, but Parker had found it amusing.

Until "Adam McCabe" became a big success.

"That's it, isn't it?" she asked out loud.

"What?"

"My success as a writer. That's what this is all about," she concluded.

"Don't be absurd!"

"It's not absurd," she argued. "You've resented my career ever since my first royalty statement arrived."

"That's not true—"

"Yes, it is," she said stubbornly. "Don't tell me it's a coincidence that you've decided to leave me the same week I signed a new contract."

"Don't flatter yourself."

"I would never have imagined in all the years I've known you, that you'd be so insecure."

"Insecure!" he snorted.

"What would you call it?" she asked. "You didn't have a problem with my career until I started earning more than you do!"

"That's absurd!" Snatching up his suitcase, he walked out without even a goodbye.

Amy's thoughts returned to the present as she looked down at the envelope in her hand. She'd once believed she and Parker were real soul mates, that they would be together forever. How wrong she'd been.

Always the cockeyed optimist, she thought sadly.

Like now... She was absolutely convinced that this letter would tell her mother that John Reynolds hadn't turned his back on her all those years ago, that he did love her, that they'd been parted by nothing more than human error.

The postal service, Amy thought ruefully. Well, at least the letter got here—even if it was over fifty years late.

She looked at the envelope again. *For Mom's sake, I have to be sure of what the letter says before I show it to her.*

Picking up a letter opener, she started to open it, then stopped herself.

I can't do this. I can't read my mother's mail. What if it's really private?

On the other hand, her mother wasn't well enough to read it herself. Amy would have to read it to her.

What if it's bad news? her conscience asked.

What if it's not? her heart responded.

"This is crazy," Amy muttered, reprimanding herself. Why would it be bad news? After all, her mother and John Reynolds had loved each other once, hadn't they? How many times had her mother talked about how much they'd meant to each other?

She wondered if they'd still been in love when this letter was written. Had he felt the same way about her mother that Marian felt about him? Amy wondered. Did true love exist?

Maybe this letter is about the future they would have had together, Amy thought, had Fate not intervened.

Only then did she stop to think about what might have been, how very different things could be—no, *would* be—had this letter been received all those years ago.

Her mother might have married John Reynolds.

Marian Haskell and Charles Barrington might never have met.

Amy might never have been born.

The thought of how one moment in time—or a letter lost in the mail—could have such a profound effect on so many people's lives fascinated Amy. Were it not for something as simple as human error, she might not even exist.

Amy spent the rest of the morning thinking about it. Since her mother had come home from the hospital a few weeks ago, she'd spent most of her waking hours recalling the past—remembering her two daughters, Amy and Patti, as children; remembering her own girlhood; remembering the man who'd been the love of her life.

Her mother had spoken fondly of John Reynolds, particularly after her husband died four years ago. She'd shown Amy all of the photographs, all of the letters she'd received from John during the war, told her stories about when he'd enlisted in the army and was sent off to Europe.

Marian had never understood why one day he'd just stopped writing. She'd wondered if he'd been killed and his family hadn't contacted her. She'd wondered if he'd met someone else, as was so common during the war, and simply forgotten about her.

It was hard to believe, and painful to accept.

But maybe he hadn't forgotten about her at all, Amy thought.

"How are you feeling, Mom?" Amy asked as she entered her mother's bedroom.

"Tired," the older woman said, frowning. "Doesn't seem like I should be tired at all, what with all the sleep I get."

"The doctor says it's to be expected," Amy reassured her, fluffing her pillows. "It'll get better."

"I think I'll go crazy if I can't leave the house anytime soon," Marian lamented as Amy put her lunch tray in front of her.

"It shouldn't be much longer," Amy said. "Which reminds me—we've got to get you a good wig."

Her mother nodded. "I suppose."

She seemed more distracted than usual, Amy thought as she positioned a chair near the bed and seated herself. "There was a letter for you in today's mail," she said softly.

"Another get well card?" her mother asked.

"No, a letter."

"From who?"

Amy hesitated, but only for a moment. "John Reynolds."

Marian dropped her fork. "John?"

"It's a very old letter," Amy said. "According to the postmark, it was mailed in 1944."

Marian thought about it for a moment. "During the war," she said.

Amy nodded.

"I thought he was dead." There were tears in her mother's eyes.

"The last letter you received from him was in mid-June," Amy reminded her. "This one was written in July."

"Took an awfully long time to get here."

Amy studied her for a moment. Her mother had definitely aged gracefully. "I'll read it to you while you eat your lunch."

Marian nodded.

Amy took the envelope from her pocket and slowly unfolded the letter. As she started to read, she looked up from time to time, searching her mother's face for clues as to what she was thinking, what she was feeling.

July 1, 1944
Dear Marian,
The longer I'm here, the more I see, the more I realize just how precious life really is. Here, we live each day knowing it might very well be our last. It makes one stop and think about how little time we have on earth, how we shouldn't waste even a minute. Which is why I'm writing now.

I love you, Marian, and being apart from you
like this has made me realize just how much I
really do love you.

I don't know what's going to happen. I don't
know if I'll be leaving here alive—but if I do
come home, if this unholy war ever ends, I hope
you'll be able to promise that I'll be coming
home to you. Say you'll be my wife, Marian.

All my love always,
John

Her mother sobbed openly. "I never knew," she
said in a raspy voice, accepting the tissues Amy offered her. "I thought he was dead. I thought he'd
changed his mind about me."

"He wanted to marry you, Mom," Amy said. "Do
you realize how different things would be today if
this letter had not been lost in the mail?"

Marian wasn't so distracted that she didn't know
what Amy was referring to. She reached out and took
her daughter's hand. "Your father was a wonderful
man," she said, "and I did love him. Don't you ever
doubt that."

Amy nodded. "I know that," she said. "But if
you'd known John wanted to marry you—"

"I don't know," Marian answered honestly. "I
think I would have waited for him."

"And you and Dad would never have met," Amy
concluded.

"I don't know that for sure," Marian insisted. "We might have met anyway—we did meet before the war was over. I might have married him anyway."

She doesn't really believe that, Amy said to herself. *She's just saying it for my sake.* What must it be like to love—and be loved—like that?

Amy lay awake that night, thinking about the day. It was a weird feeling, knowing that if not for a simple mistake on the part of a total stranger, she might never have been born.

Would her parents have met anyway? Possibly.

Would they have still gotten married? Amy didn't think so.

Would her mother and John Reynolds have eventually gotten married? The odds were in favor of it.

Would that marriage have lasted? Hard to tell.

What would their children have been like? Amy wondered. It made her think. What did happen to John Reynolds? Did he survive the war? Did he return to the States? Did he marry? Did he have any children? Was he still alive? Did he ever think about what might have been?

The questions were endless.

Amy thought about her mother, about the difference John Reynolds's letter had made. She'd really perked up. Imagine how she would have reacted if he'd shown up at the door in the flesh.

She wondered where John was now. Did he ever think about her mother?

Surely he hasn't forgotten. He'd wanted to marry her, after all.

Marian still thought about him, wondered about what might have been. Amy found it hard to believe that John Reynolds didn't still think about her, as well.

Amy remembered her mother saying—more than once, actually—that John Reynolds came from a small coastal town in Maine called Burke's Harbor. Her mother had said he'd wanted to settle there after the war. Maybe he had.

If Amy could find him and bring him here, it could very well be the best medicine her mother could possibly have....

This is crazy, she told herself. She couldn't just call him—well, obviously she couldn't call him, she didn't have his phone number, though she could probably get it. What would she say? "Hi, there, you almost married my mother!"

Definitely not a good idea.

Mom had married someone else; he probably had, too. And since he'd never been given a response, he'd probably thought he'd been dumped, too.

Suddenly her mind drifted to her father. Had he known about John Reynolds? If so, he'd never mentioned it. But then, it was hardly the sort of thing he would have discussed with his wife in front of their two daughters.

Would it have bothered him?

Amy had to believe it hadn't. Whatever her mother felt—had felt—over the years for John Reynolds, her parents had had a good marriage. They'd been happy together.

She was sure of it.

She didn't sleep at all that night. By the time the sun rose over Boston Harbor, Amy had reached a decision. She was going to try to find John Reynolds.

She didn't think she would be hurting her father or his memory by doing so, either. In fact, she felt certain he would understand that she was only trying to help her mother.

Amy got out of bed and put on a robe. Moving as quietly as she could, she went to the office she'd set up in one of the guest rooms and took out a road atlas, flipping through the pages until she found the map for the state of Maine. She ran her index finger along the coastline until she found what she was looking for.

Burke's Harbor. Just west of Kennebunkport.

Nice area. Very nice. Maybe a two-hour drive.

She picked up the phone on her desk and dialed her sister's number in Hyannisport.

When Patti came on the line, she sounded groggy. "Hullo?"

"Patti, it's Amy."

"Amy? Do you know what time it is?"

"I know it's early, but I wouldn't be calling if it weren't urgent," Amy insisted.

Suddenly, Patti was alarmed. "Mom. Is she all right?"

"Mom's fine," Amy assured her. "It's nothing like that."

"What then? And this had better be good."

"I need you to come up and stay with her for a while," Amy said. "I have to go out of town."

"Business?"

"Yes—business." Amy decided it would be best not to tell Patti where she was going or why—at least not yet. She wasn't going to tell her mother yet, either.

No point in risking disappointing her again if Amy couldn't find him—or he didn't want to see her after so much time had passed.

"When do you want to leave?" Patti asked.

"As soon as possible."

"I can get up there sometime tomorrow, then."

"Thanks, Pats."

As soon as she hung up, she returned to her bedroom to start packing.

2

Burke's Harbor, Maine

"**Y**ou look tired," Katie Kirk observed as her brother entered the bed and breakfast she owned.

Brian Reynolds shook his head. "I don't know how much more I can take," he admitted wearily.

"Dad again?"

"You'd think at his age he wouldn't be able to get around well enough to be a problem," Brian said, exasperated. "I hope I'm that energetic when I'm his age."

Katie's smile was disbelieving. "He's not *that* old, Bri," she reminded him.

"Old enough," he maintained. "And with a bad leg, to boot."

"What are you two going at it about now?" Katie asked as she closed the reservation book and got up from her seat at the hall desk.

"Anything and everything," he said with a snort. "You name it, we fight about it."

"Maybe Dad should move in with Jerry and me," Katie suggested.

Brian shook his head. "We've been through this before, Katie," he said wearily. "You know as well as I do, he'll never agree to that."

"I can't imagine him wanting to go on living with you—not the way things have been going between the two of you," Katie responded.

"He wants to stay in his own home," Brian reminded her.

"And you just happen to be there," Katie concluded.

"Exactly." He paused. "Is that fresh coffee I smell?"

She laughed. "Like you even have to ask. Want a cup?"

He followed her into the large, country-style kitchen. She took two cups from the cupboard and poured the steaming hot coffee. "Are you always going to come here for your morning coffee?" she asked, teasing.

He shrugged as he took a seat at the table. "Easier than making it at home."

"Don't you really mean that it's easier than having to have breakfast with Dad?" Katie replaced the coffeepot and moved toward the table, a cup in each hand.

He didn't answer at first. "Maybe," he said finally, taking the cup Katie held out to him.

"Why do you hate him so, Bri?" she asked, sitting across from him.

He looked genuinely surprised by the question. "I don't hate him," he insisted.

"You could have fooled me."

"I don't. We just don't see eye-to-eye, that's all," he answered evasively.

"That's an understatement if I ever heard one."

"That's all there is to it."

She looked unconvinced. "This has been going on since he and Mom split up," she stated.

He drew in a deep breath. "All right, so I don't hide my feelings well."

"What's the real problem?" Katie asked.

"I haven't been able to forget what he did to Mom," Brian admitted.

"Mom left him, Bri. Not the other way around," she reminded him.

"She left because he didn't love her!" he snapped.

"That's not true!"

"He was in love with someone else," Brian said. "You know that as well as I do."

"Oh, come on—that was a long time ago," Katie said. "That was during the war, before he even met Mom."

"He never got over her."

"How do you know that?"

"Mom knew it. Why do you think she left?" He

was bitter and not trying to hide it. He resented his father's inability to love his mother.

"That's unfair, Brian," she told him. "Some couples just don't belong together. Mom and Dad didn't. It happens."

He scowled at her. "And you wonder why I never married again after Elaine died!"

"You've never married again because you haven't met another woman who could put up with you," Katie said, half teasing.

"Funny." He finished his coffee. "Got to go," he said as he got to his feet.

"What's your hurry?"

He grinned. "Wouldn't you like to know?"

"Brian, you louse!" she called after him as he departed.

Driving north along the Atlantic coast on such a beautiful May afternoon, Amy normally would have been in awe of the magnificent scenery—but not this time. This time, her mind was on other things.

Today her mission was to find John Reynolds.

Her sister would think she was nuts. Her friends would think she was nuts. Just about everyone she knew would think she was nuts.

Except her mother. Her mother would understand.

Her mother would understand her fascination with the letter, with the lives of two people irrevocably changed by a mistake, of the lives that would never have existed, had that letter been delivered.

Does he still think of Mom the way she still thinks of him?

Does he still care?

Is he still alive?

What do I do if he is alive? she asked herself. *What do I say to him? I guess that depends on whether or not he's married.*

Mom's widowed. Maybe he is, too. She paused. She should be ashamed of herself for wishing such a thing.

But wouldn't it be wonderful for Mom?

She arrived in Burke's Harbor early in the evening. With a brief stop at the first gas station she came upon, she was able to obtain the name of the town's only bed and breakfast. Twenty minutes later, she was checked in and shown to her room.

"If you need anything, just let me know. Dinner, maybe?" she was told by the friendly, energetic woman who showed her to her room. "I'm Katie Kirk. I own this establishment."

Amy smiled. "Thank you."

"Business or pleasure?"

"Excuse me?"

"Your visit to Burke's Harbor, business or pleasure?" Katie clarified her question.

"It's not exactly either one," Amy admitted.

Katie gave her a quizzical look.

"I'm looking for someone," Amy explained.

Katie grinned. "Shouldn't be hard to find—this is a really small town."

"I hope you're right," Amy said. "My mother's been very ill. If I can find this person, it could make all the difference in the world to her."

"Sounds important," Katie said. "I might be able to help. I've lived here all my life."

Amy nodded. "I'd appreciate it," she said gratefully. "This man—the person I'm looking for—is someone my mother knew years ago. Someone she was deeply in love with."

"What happened?" Katie asked.

"She thought she'd been dumped," Amy told her. "One day, it just ended. She never heard from him again. She assumed he'd found someone else."

"She never tried to find him?" Katie asked as she turned down the bed and checked the drawers and closet.

Amy shook her head. "There was no reason to," she said. "She believed she'd been dumped."

"But she wasn't?"

"No," Amy said. "He'd written her a letter—a marriage proposal, actually. It would have been perfect if it hadn't gotten lost in the mail."

"Sounds terribly romantic."

"Doesn't it?"

"What about your father?" Katie asked then.

"What about him?" Amy asked, not quite sure she understood.

"How does he feel about—"

"He never knew," Amy replied. "My parents had a good marriage. They loved each other. But I think my mother always wondered what might have been."

Katie was silent for a moment. "If his letter was lost in the mail," she began, "how did you find out about it?"

"That's the weird part," said Amy. "The letter that was lost in the mail was finally delivered this week."

Katie looked intrigued, waiting for her to go on with the story.

"More than fifty years after it was mailed, it was finally delivered," Amy said again. "Mom hasn't been home from the hospital very long—she's had brain surgery—and she wasn't doing well. My father died four years ago, and she wasn't happy about being alone. That letter boosted her spirits as nothing else could have."

"The man," Katie said then. "What was his name? Maybe I know him."

"Reynolds. John Reynolds."

"Where's Dad?"

Brian gave Katie a curious once-over. "What did you do, run all the way from the B and B?"

"Where is he?"

"Not here," Brian said. "We had another fight. He got ticked off and left."

"You let him leave alone?"

"He's a grown man, Katie," he said. "What's this all about, anyway?"

"There's a woman staying at my place."

Brian grinned. "Don't you think he's a little old for that sort of thing?" he asked.

"I'm serious, Brian!"

"So am I," he insisted. "You want the old guy to have a coronary?"

"You don't understand."

"Okay," he said promptly. "Make me understand."

"This woman came all the way from Boston to find a man her mother knew years ago," Katie told him. "They were lovers before the war. He sent her a marriage proposal by mail when he was stationed in Europe. It was lost in the mail—the woman believed she'd been dumped."

"Touching," he said without much interest.

"The letter reached her this week," Katie said.

"So?"

"Her father's dead. Her mother's alone now," Katie went on. "She recently had major surgery."

"Why does all of this upset you so much?" Brian asked curiously.

Katie's eyes met his. "The man she's looking for

is our father," she said. "Her mother is the woman he wanted to marry before he met our mother."

"Can't be," he said, shaking his head emphatically.

"Why do you say that?"

"Dad loved that woman so much, she came between him and Mom," Brian reminded her. "He believed *she* dumped him. He would never have dumped her!"

"Don't you see what's happened?" she asked. "The letter—his proposal—was lost in the mail. She never received it. She thought he dumped her. Because she didn't get it, she didn't give him an answer—so he thought she dumped him."

"All of a sudden this woman appears out of the blue—fifty years later. You think this woman is legit?" he asked, unbelieving.

"I'm surprised you don't."

"How so?"

"For one thing, you're the one who's had a chip the size of Rhode Island on his shoulder about this from the time you found out about Dad's first love," she told him.

"I still find it hard to believe she's come looking for him now, after all these years," he said stubbornly.

"You didn't find it so hard to believe that Dad was still carrying a torch after all these years," she said.

"That was a little too obvious not to believe," he said darkly. "Did you tell her—"

Katie shook her head. "She took me by surprise," she said. "She told me the name of the man she was looking for as I was walking out the door."

"Then she doesn't know?"

"Not yet. Why?"

"Don't tell her."

"Don't be absurd," she chided. "It's up to Dad to decide whether or not he wants to see this woman."

Brian made a face. "You know what he'll say."

"He'll want to see her."

"Of course he will!"

"If he does," Katie said, "it's up to him."

"Katie—"

"It's his decision, Brian. *His*—not ours."

Unfortunately, Brian thought, she was right.

Will he remember? Amy wondered.

It was one of those nights. Under normal conditions, she would be asleep the moment her head hit the pillow—literally—and sleep soundly until morning. At times like these, though, when she had a problems to resolve, she found sleep difficult.

Like tonight.

Of course he'll remember, she assured herself. The kind of love he and her mother had shared is rare. He wouldn't forget. He couldn't forget.

If he's still alive.

She turned over in the bed, facing the window. It was a clear night, lots of stars brightening the sky. The moon was full. Through the partially open window, the salty smell of the Atlantic Ocean filled the room.

This was like being on a houseboat, she decided. Without the waves.

She thought about her conversation earlier with Katie Kirk. The big, rambling, Victorian house she'd turned into what appeared to be a most popular bed and breakfast reflected the warmth and friendliness of the woman who ran it.

She said she might be able to help her. She hoped so.

She hoped she hadn't made this trip for nothing.

But it wouldn't be for nothing. If John Reynolds *was* dead, she obviously couldn't reunite him with her mother. Still, there was bound to be someone still living in Burke's Harbor who knew him, who could tell her something about him.

Like what happened to him, she thought. Like what he did after the war.

If he'd married.

If he'd had any children.

If he'd ever thought about her mother.

It was late, almost 2:00 a.m., but she decided to place a call to Boston anyway. Switching on the bedside lamp, she took her calling card from her wallet—

she'd never been able to remember her card num-ber—and dialed.

Her sister answered. "Hello?"

"Patti?"

"Amy?"

"Yeah, it's me."

"I'm buying you a watch for Christmas."

"Huh?"

"Obviously you don't already own one."

"Sorry about the time, Pats," Amy apologized. "How's Mom?"

"Sleeping. I wish I were."

"I am sorry," Amy insisted. "I just kept thinking about her. I wanted to make sure she was all right."

"She's fine," Patti reassured her sister. "She saw the doctor today. He says she's doing fine."

"That's a relief."

"Where are you, anyway?" Patti wanted to know.

"Maine," Amy answered evasively. She wasn't ready to tell Patti what she was up to. Not yet. "I'm...doing some research." She gave her sister the telephone number of the Kirks' Bed and Breakfast. "You can reach me here if you need me."

"Don't worry about Mom, Amy," Patti said, sti-fling a yawn. "She's a lot tougher than she looks."

Amy gave a little laugh, not sure she agreed. "Give her a kiss for me, okay?"

"I will," Patti promised. "When will you be home, Amy?"

"I don't know," she confessed. "Soon, I hope."

And, she hoped, not empty-handed.

"I've been worried about you," Brian said as his father came through the front door as the clock on the mantel chimed nine-thirty.

The elder Reynolds scowled at him. "I'll bet."

Brian was exasperated. His father often had that effect on him. "Dad, whether you believe it or not, I do care about you," he said.

"You'll excuse me if I don't take that on faith," John huffed as he made his way to his favorite chair, a worn-out leather recliner.

Brian didn't respond at first. "This isn't working," he said finally.

"There's a news flash."

"Katie wants you to move in with her and Jerry. Maybe you should."

"Maybe you should move," John retorted sharply. "This is my house, remember?"

"Maybe I will."

"Don't let the door hit your butt on the way out, boy," John advised.

The old guy could be so infuriating sometimes. Brian decided it would be better to leave than to stay and argue with him, so he went out onto the porch and sat on the railing, staring up at the clear night sky.

Where did we go wrong? he asked himself, as he had so many times before.

But he already knew the answer.

He resented his father for the problems with his mother. His father knew it.

When he was a boy, they'd been close, so close. He'd been his father's shadow—wherever John Reynolds went, Brian Reynolds was never very far behind. Whatever his father did, he wanted to do. He never thought anything would ever come between them.

Until the day his mother told him about the divorce.

How could you do that to her, Dad? How could you hurt her like that, knowing how much she loved you?

How could you hurt us?

Brian wished he were more like Katie. She'd handled the divorce well. Sometimes he thought she'd handled it too well. There were times he wondered if she really cared if their parents were together or not.

Katie has her own family now, he reminded himself. Her own kids, her own life. Maybe that makes a difference.

Maybe if he had his own family, he would feel differently.

He thought about the things Katie had said to him. She didn't find their father entirely to blame for the breakup of the marriage. She loved their father. She wanted him to be happy.

I love him, too. I really do, Brian kept telling himself.

But I love Mom, too.

And I can't just forget how deeply he hurt her, can I?

If I could forget, maybe I could have a normal relationship with a woman.

Maybe I could make someone happy...happier than I was able to make Elaine when she was alive.

Maybe I could believe in love.

Maybe I could believe in relationships.

Then he thought of his mother again, and the pain his father had caused her.

How will she feel if Dad ends up reunited with that woman?

But in the end, Katie was right, he conceded. Their father was a grown man. He had the right to make his own decisions, no matter how Brian felt about those decisions.

If I keep this from him, it'll only make things worse between us, he thought.

He went back into the house. "Dad, we need to talk," he told his father.

John Reynolds didn't look up from the newspaper he'd been reading.

"Dad?"

John's only response was a soft snoring sound. He had fallen asleep, the newspaper still clutched in his outstretched hands.

Ah, well, Brian thought almost with relief as he slowly backed out of the room. This news has kept for better than fifty years, what's a few more hours?

3

"Amy, this is my brother, Brian," Katie said, knocking on Amy's open door. "Brian *Reynolds*."

"Reynolds?" Amy turned from the view out her bedroom window to look at the man, then at Katie. "John Reynolds is—"

"*Our* father," Brian supplied as he moved into the center of the room.

"Your father." Amy nodded her head in confusion as she sank slowly into a nearby chair. "John Reynolds is your father." Half question, half statement.

Brian nodded.

She turned her eyes to Katie who was standing at the front of the bed. "Why didn't you tell me?" she asked. "I told you the whole story, right here in this room. Why didn't you tell me last night that John Reynolds was your father?"

"You didn't tell me the identity of the man you were looking for until I was walking out the door," Katie said honestly.

"But I *did* tell you. And you never said a word."

"She thought she'd better talk to me first," Brian explained, defending his sister.

Amy said nothing, waiting for him to go on.

"She knows how I feel about all of this."

"Then you already knew about..." Amy began, genuinely surprised.

"About our father and your mother?" The look on his face was puzzling to Amy. "We've known for years."

"Since we were children," Katie agreed, nodding as she moved to stand near her brother.

"Your father told you—"

"He didn't have to," Brian interjected tightly. "We picked up on it from all the arguments he and our mother had about it over the years."

"Arguments?" Amy felt the color drain from her face. While she hadn't known what to expect when she'd embarked on this quest, the last thing she'd anticipated, in all the possible scenarios she'd played out in her mind, was open hostility.

But that's exactly what she'd run into here.

"Let's just say our mother was less than thrilled about it," Brian said.

"Your mother?"

"*Our* mother," he repeated. "John Reynolds's ex-wife."

Now Amy was really uncomfortable. "Is your father still alive?" she asked, hoping to change the subject, however slightly.

Katie nodded.

"He's too mean to die." Brian seemed to regret having come to talk to her at all.

"Is he…" She wasn't sure she should ask.

"Is he married now?" Brian asked, guessing what the rest of her question was going to be. "No, he isn't. Our parents divorced years ago. I guess our father decided not to make the same mistake twice."

Amy opted to not even open that for discussion, curious as she was. "Would you mind—could I meet him?" she asked hesitantly.

Brian and Katie looked at each other.

"Would he be willing to talk to me?" She hadn't come this far to just give up now.

"I think so," Katie said.

"He doesn't know you're here—yet." Brian paused. "Why is it so important that you see him, Ms. Barrington? Why now, after all these years?"

"I told your sister." Amy stood. "My mother recently underwent a serious operation. Brain surgery. We didn't know if she was going to make it or not."

"I'm sorry about that, but what does it have to do with—"

"I'm getting to that," Amy assured him. "After my father died, my mother told my sister and me about your father, about how much she'd loved him—"

"If she loved him so much, why did she just drop

him without so much as an explanation?'' Brian wanted to know.

"She didn't!"

"That's not the way my father tells it."

"He sent my mother a letter—a marriage proposal, actually—while he was in Europe during the war," Amy said. "The letter was lost in the mail—until this week. When it came, Mom was so moved—all these years, to find out he hadn't dumped her after all, that he had wanted to marry her."

"He thinks she didn't want to marry him," Brian declared. "That she just chose not to answer his letter at all."

"If I could talk to him—"

"We'll see, Ms. Barrington," he said as he turned and motioned for Katie to follow him from the room.

"What's the matter?" Katie asked when they reached the B and B's great room.

"Nothing," Brian responded, his back to her as he stared out the window.

"Right."

He hadn't expected to feel the way he did when he came face-to-face with Marian Haskell's daughter for the first time. Actually, he wasn't exactly sure what he did feel. He was still sorting that out in his own mind.

Given what he knew about Marian Haskell, the woman he'd just met upstairs came as a real surprise.

Not at all what he would have expected. He would have guessed her daughter to be more perfect somehow—more prim and proper. More ladylike. Amy Barrington was anything but prim and proper.

Sexy. That was the word he would use to describe her. Not blatantly sexy, not by a long shot, but sexy nonetheless. Long blond hair, straight to the shoulders; wide blue eyes. Spunky, definitely spunky. *Not my type,* he thought.

Still, he was intrigued....

He's an attractive man, Amy thought somewhat begrudgingly later that morning. That scowl detracts from his looks, but he's still one good-looking guy.

Probably knows it, too.

He looked like his father—at least, he looked like the photographs she'd seen of his father as a young man. Tall, blond hair, boyishly handsome.

Except John Reynolds was almost always smiling. The smile made a big difference.

It seemed Brian Reynolds had disliked her on sight, and that puzzled Amy. How could anyone dislike another human being on sight? She'd always been willing to give anybody a chance.

Except in the romance department, of course. She'd just never met the right man, that was all.

Everybody has their limits, she told herself.

She wondered what Brian Reynolds's limit might be.

* * *

"His daughter owns the bed and breakfast, and his son…well, his son's another story," Amy told Patti when she called back to confess her real reason for being in Burke's Harbor.

"What's that supposed to mean?"

"You'd have to meet him yourself to believe it, really."

"Try me."

Amy sighed heavily. "He's maybe a few years older than me, tall, good-looking—though he'd probably be a lot better looking if he'd smile once in a while," she told her sister. "He's blond, looks like the type who spends a lot of time on a boat, if you know what I mean. As a matter of fact, I think he runs some kind of boat charter service. That's what I've heard around the B and B, anyway."

"That's not what I mean and you know it."

"He acts like I've committed a crime or something just by being here," Amy said. "I think it's going to take an act of congress for me to get anywhere near John Reynolds."

"You exaggerate."

"Not this time, Pats."

"Do you want me to tell Mom you've found him?" Patti asked.

"Better not—at least not yet," Amy cautioned. "Wait until I see him—if I get to see him."

"All right. I guess that would be the best way to handle this situation," Patti agreed.

"I'll let you know if I get past the palace guard," Amy promised.

"Do that."

After she hung up, Amy lay back on her bed, arms folded behind her head, thinking. This Brian Reynolds was some piece of work, that was for sure. If the father was anything like the son—no, that wasn't possible. If the father were even remotely like the son, her mother wouldn't have looked at him twice.

Sure, he's good-looking, Amy thought, but he's also an insufferable jerk...to put it mildly.

No, John Reynolds couldn't possibly be anything like his son. If his letters to her mother were any indication, the elder Reynolds was a kind, caring, deeply romantic man.

Too bad she couldn't say the same for his son.

Pulling her soft-sided briefcase from under the bed, she opened it and took out a bundle of very old letters tied together with a narrow red ribbon. She untied the ribbon and opened one of the letters, reading it once more to remind herself of the kind of man John Reynolds was....

Dec. 15, 1943
My darling Marian,
It's not going to be a very merry Christmas for those of us stuck over here during the holidays.

We'll just have to make the best of a bad situation—though I'm not quite sure how.

The only thing that's getting me through these endless days and nights here is you—thoughts of you and the wonderful times we shared in New York, the letters I get from you, the promise of what we have to look forward to when the war is over.

I'm in Paris now—what a place it must have been before the occupation! Walking down the Champs-Elysées the other day with members of the Resistance—I wish I could explain, but I can't, not yet—I found myself thinking of you....

"You shouldn't be here," he told her.

"Did you think I'd be anywhere else?" she asked, *trying to look into his eyes but unable to do so because the wide-brimmed hat he wore shadowed his face. "No,* mon cher, *my place is here, with you, fighting by your side."*

She was dressed like Ingrid Bergman in the airport scene from the movie *Casablanca*. Come to think of it, this dream was in black and white. Black, white and shades of gray, if fog counted. She'd never dreamed in black and white before.

"I couldn't bear it if anything happened to you," he said, turning away. *"You have the papers. I want you to leave. Now. Today."*

"Don't ask me to leave you behind, because I can't," she insisted stubbornly.

"You must."

She shook her head emphatically. *"The cause needs us both."*

"You can do more for me—and the cause—in Washington," he declared, pressuring her.

"You're only telling me that because you want me to leave!" she cried.

"I want you to be safe!" he argued. *"How am I supposed to keep a clear head, to do what has to be done, if I'm always thinking about you, always worried that you could be in danger?"*

"You'll know that I'm not if I'm always with you."

"You are, without a doubt, the most infuriatingly stubborn woman I've ever known!" he exhorted as he turned away from her.

She grasped his shoulders and summoned up all the strength she could to turn him around to face her.

"I learned from the master!" she cried, pulling the hat back so she could kiss him.

It was then that she realized the man beneath the hat was Brian Reynolds—

Amy woke with a start, relieved to discover it was only a dream. "I should have known," she muttered. "Brian Reynolds and I are hardly the Bogart and Bergman type."

Silently she admitted, *we don't even like each other.*

"Well...are you going to let her talk to him or not?" Katie wanted to know.

"That's going to have to be his decision." Brian didn't look at her as they walked from the bed and breakfast through town to their father's home, followed by Katie's kids.

Katie was unable to hide her surprise. "You're actually going to tell him?" she asked.

"I started to tell him last night," Brian admitted. "He came in not long after you left. But we got into another argument, and I went outside to cool off. When I went back inside, he was asleep in the chair."

"I don't like it," Katie told him. "I don't like the idea of him taking off by himself for long periods of time, not bothering to tell anyone where he's going."

"I don't like it, either," he said quietly, "but short of locking him in his room and posting a guard at the front door, I don't know how to stop him."

"I wondered where you got it."

"What?"

"Never mind." She waved him off. "Do you want me to be there when you tell him?"

"You can be there if you want to," he answered. "Makes no difference to me either way."

"Thanks."

"No offense intended."

"None taken."

"He'll want to see her, you know," Brian stated after a brief silence.

"Amy?"

"No. Her mother," he elaborated. "He'll want to see her mother."

"You really think so? After all these years?" Katie asked dubiously.

"I'm sure of it," he said. "That's all he's ever wanted, to be reunited with his long-lost love."

"Still, it *has* been over fifty years—"

"Doesn't matter—not to Dad, anyway," he said. "All he's ever really cared about is that woman."

"That's not true!" Katie disagreed. "He cares about us!"

"Maybe, to an extent."

"You don't make it easy for him to care about you, Bri," his sister admonished.

"I don't think he's ever really tried," Brian responded defensively.

"When did you ever give him a chance?" she asked. "As a child, you turned away from him, blaming him for Mother's unhappiness—"

"He *was* to blame!"

"When a marriage fails, it's almost never the fault of just one of the parties involved," Katie noted patiently.

"It was in their case."

"And you wonder why he can't reach out to you,"

she said. "No matter how much he might care, that wall is always going to be there between you—because you won't let it come down."

She turned and headed back to the bed and breakfast, leaving her brother staring after her.

"Dad?"

Brian called out to his father as he entered the house, but there was no response. In fact, there was no sign of life whatsoever in the big, empty house.

This house has always been empty, he thought as he went to the kitchen for a glass of ice water. Always. Even when we were all at home, it always seemed empty.

In his mind, he could see the home of his childhood, such as it had been—his father sitting there, in what was still his favorite chair, watching TV or reading his newspaper; his mother, knitting or reading a book—she loved novels, loved the mental escape they provided; he and Katie, preteens, sitting on the floor playing a board game, cards, or something like that.

Everyone in the same room, but no warmth, no emotional connection, he thought sadly. *Except maybe between Katie and me.*

His mother and father could spend the entire day in the same room and never acknowledge each other. And those were the good days.

On the not-so-good days, when they did acknowledge each other's presence, it was almost always in the form of a bitter argument. His parents' relationship had always been one of extremes—icy silence or heated verbal warfare.

He took his glass and went back into the living room, where he settled down on the couch to wait for his father. This ought to make him happy, he thought. Finally he'll get what he's always wanted.

He'll get to see her again.

Or will he?

Surely Amy Barrington had not come here simply to find his father and tell him her mother had finally received the marriage proposal he'd mailed to her fifty years ago. No...there had to be more to it than that.

He was definitely curious about that one. Amy Barrington was young, attractive, and as far as he could tell, bright—surely she had better things to do than go chasing after a man her mother had been in love with half a century ago. Didn't she have a career to occupy her time, or a husband and children?

The sound of the front door slamming cut through his thoughts. He looked up to see his father. ''Where have you been?'' he asked a little too sharply.

''What are you, my keeper?'' John took off his cap and put it on the coatrack near the door.

''Don't be so defensive,'' Brian protested. ''I'm not keeping tabs on you.''

''Sure, you're not.''

"All right, maybe I do sometimes," Brian conceded. "But not this time."

"No?" John gave him a curious look. "What's different about this time?"

"We were trying to find you—"

"We?"

"Katie and me."

"Why?"

"There's someone in town looking for you," Brian told him.

"For me? That hasn't happened in a long time," he commented.

"A woman."

John smiled. "That definitely hasn't happened in a long time."

"I'm serious."

"Aren't you always?"

"This woman is young, pretty—"

"Doesn't sound like anybody who'd be looking for me," John said with an offhanded shrug.

"She's from Boston."

John stopped in his tracks. "Boston?"

Brian nodded. "Her name is Amy Barrington," he said quietly.

"Doesn't sound familiar," John said, shaking his head.

"Her mother's name is Marian Haskell Barrington."

4

"**M**arian?" John was stunned.

Brian nodded. "This young woman is her daughter," he said.

"Daughter." John moved slowly as he sank into his chair. "She had a daughter."

"Two, I think."

John nodded numbly. "She did marry, then."

"Her daughter says she's a widow," Brian revealed.

"She's still alive, then?"

Brian nodded again.

"What brings her daughter here to Burke's Harbor?" John asked curiously.

Brian frowned. "You."

"Me? But why—"

"Her mother got your letter."

John looked confused. "I didn't send any letter..." he began.

"The one you sent fifty years ago," Brian clarified. "The marriage proposal you sent during the war."

"Are you saying—"

"She just got it. This week, I believe." Brian thought that was what Amy had said, though he wasn't sure.

"This week!"

"Something like that, yeah."

John was silent awhile. "She just got it. After all these years," he said slowly. "That explains everything."

Brian drew in a deep breath. "It explains why you didn't end up married to her, why you had to settle for my mother instead."

"Brian—"

He raised a hand to silence his father. "Don't worry, that's all I'm going to say," he promised. "No point in beating a dead horse."

"Did she want to see me?" John asked.

"What?" Brian had been lost in his own bitter thoughts.

"Marian's daughter. She came here to see me, didn't she?"

"Yes, she did." Brian pulled himself upright. "I think she wants to take you to her mother."

John looked at him, surprised. "Take me to her?"

"She's in Boston, recovering from brain surgery," Brian said.

John didn't try to hide his concern. "Brain surgery?"

"I don't know all the details," Brian told him. "I only spoke to her briefly, earlier today."

"She's at Katie's?"

Brian nodded.

"So when can I talk to her?" he asked.

Brian paused. "Now, if you want to," he said finally.

John nodded. "I want to." He headed for the door.

"Wait a minute!" Brian called after him. "Let me call Katie to make sure Amy hasn't gone out!"

What made me think he might not want to see her? Brian asked himself.

They'll be here any minute now, Amy thought.

Ever since Katie had called up to her room to tell Amy that Brian would be bringing their father to meet her after dinner, she had been trying to imagine what he was like, what meeting him was going to be like.

What kind of man was he? From what her mother had told her about him, he had to be something pretty special. Out of the ordinary.

Certainly not like the men I've known, she thought. *They don't make 'em like that anymore, I guess. At least I haven't found any.*

Her mother had been so lucky, so very lucky. She'd had two wonderful men in her life, two men who truly loved her.

I would have been satisfied with just one, she thought.

* * *

"This is my father, John Reynolds," Brian said as the elder Reynolds stepped forward.

Amy moved from her position at the entrance to the B and B's great room to shake hands with the older man. "I'm very happy to meet you, Mr. Reynolds," she told him.

"Please, call me John." He was grinning from ear to ear.

She nodded. "John."

"You look like her."

"I beg your pardon?"

"Your mother. You look a lot like her," John said. "Same eyes, same mouth—only her hair was darker."

"My father was blond."

He nodded, obviously taken with her. "Looking at you now brings back a lot of memories," he confessed. "Makes me think of how Marian looked the last time I saw her."

"I know," Amy said softly. "I've seen old photographs of her."

"Except she wouldn't be caught dead in leather," he added with a grin, noting her attire.

Amy laughed. "If she'd tried, my grandparents would most certainly have done something about it."

"How is she?" John asked, concern edging his voice. "My son tells me she had brain surgery."

Amy nodded. "She's doing very well, thank you." Then she added, "She'd very much like to see you."

"I'd like to see her, too."

She smiled. "I was hoping you'd say that."

"Brian says she just got my letter," John said. "Pretty hard to believe."

"But true," Amy assured him. "I'll never forget the day the mailman delivered it. I was stunned."

Brian, seated in one of the large armchairs in Katie's great room, said nothing, just looked on in silence, observing the exchange with mixed feelings. He would have given just about anything, anything in the world, if his father had said, "No, I don't think there's anything to be gained by seeing her now, after all these years."

He's still in love with her, even now, Brian thought miserably. *Mother was right. He never got over Marian.*

Brian resigned himself to the fact that he would be taking his father to Boston to see this woman, much as he hated the idea. John was going to go, with or without him. If Brian refused to take him, it would only make things worse between them.

"Don't you think so, Brian?"

It took Brian a moment to realize that Amy was talking to him. "What?"

"I was just telling your father it would probably be best to leave early tomorrow morning," she explained.

"And I think there's no point in wasting time," John growled. "No reason not to leave right away."

Brian straightened. "Look, Dad, I know how eager you are to see this woman again..." he started to say, hoping he didn't sound too sarcastic. "But I have to agree with Ms. Barrington, here. It doesn't make much sense to try to drive it tonight."

"I've already waited fifty years," John grumbled, annoyed with both of them and not bothering to hide it.

"Nobody knows that better than I do, Dad," Brian assured him.

"After waiting all that time, one more day shouldn't be so tough," Amy reasoned.

"At my age, days count," he told her. "Hours count...heck, even minutes count!"

In the end, though, he gave in.

Brian couldn't help but wonder where all of this might lead.

Never in his wildest dreams had he imagined that this would or even could happen. Who could have predicted that the great love of his father's life would so suddenly resurface?

He certainly couldn't have, and he'd lived with the specter of their great romance all his life.

Immediately upon their return to the house, his father had gone to his room to pack a bag for their trip to Boston. He wanted to see Marian—not that this came as any great surprise. Seeing her, being with her, was all he'd ever wanted, even during all the years he'd been married to Brian's mother.

He would have left Mom for her in a heartbeat, Brian thought now. *He would have left all of us.*

That was what bothered him most—believing, for as long as he could remember, that his father might leave them at any time. That if this woman who meant so much to him were to come back into his life, he would abandon his wife and children without so much as a second thought. Brian was, deep within his soul, still that scared little boy who'd spent too many nights crying himself to sleep, hiding his head under his pillow, trying to block out the painful sounds of his parents' nasty arguments.

It would take more than a lifetime to forget that. If he ever could.

"You married?" John asked, looking at Amy from his position beside her in the passenger seat.

It was early morning and the three of them were en route to Boston in Amy's car. Brian had planned to drive, following Amy in her car, since Amy wasn't planning to return to Burke's Harbor, but when the time came to leave, his truck had engine problems, so he'd reluctantly agreed to ride with Amy. He told her he would rent a car for the return trip.

"No," Amy said to John. "Not anymore."

"Divorced?"

"Mmm-hmm."

"Any kids?"

"Unfortunately, no."

"You like kids?"

"I love children," Amy told him.

"Dad, don't you think you're being just a little bit too nosy?" Brian cut in from the back seat.

"Nothing wrong with a little healthy curiosity," John insisted, turning his head to look at Brian. "You should try it sometime, Brian."

"I don't mind, really," Amy said.

"See?" John told more than asked his son. "She doesn't mind, so why should you?"

Brian waved him off. "Okay, Dad—I stand corrected." He sighed.

John turned back to Amy. "What do you do for a living?"

"I'm a writer."

"TV or movies?"

"Neither," Amy said. "I write books. Mystery novels, actually."

Brian showed interest in their conversation for the first time. "A mystery writer—really?" he asked.

She nodded. "You like mysteries?"

"They're his favorite form of literature," John told her.

"Do you write under your own name?" Brian asked.

"No—which is probably why it doesn't sound familiar to you," she said, amused by the embarrassment on his face. "The type of book I write is, according to my publisher, much too hard-boiled to have been written by a woman, so I had to come up with a male pseudonym."

"Which is?"

"Adam McCabe."

He couldn't hide his surprise. "*You're* Adam McCabe?" he asked, amazed.

She laughed. "In the flesh, so to speak," she told him.

"I think I've read everything you've ever done," Brian admitted.

"I take it you like my books, then?"

"That's an understatement if I ever heard one," John chuckled.

"Very much," Brian said, nodding.

"But?"

"But never in a million years would I have guessed that Adam McCabe was a...a..."

"Woman," Amy supplied.

"Well...yes." The understatement of the year. Not just a woman—a beautiful, sexy woman.

"I'm not sure quite how to take that," she said, trying not to laugh. This was going to be a fun trip after all, she decided. She was really starting to like this man.

"I didn't mean to be insulting," he assured her. "It's just that you don't write like a woman."

"Oh? How does a woman write?"

"Well, you know——" He felt more than a little embarrassed.

"No, I don't know," she insisted. "Tell me."

"Women tend to be more romantic, more optimistic," he attempted to explain. "More emotional."

"That's not my style," she said.

"Obviously." Does she mean professionally—or personally? he wondered.

"You never guessed, really?"

"Huh?"

"You never even suspected that Adam McCabe wasn't really a man?"

"Not even for a minute."

"That's great!"

"Yeah?"

"Yeah," she said with a nod. "My publisher owes me dinner at Lutecé."

"What's that got to do with——" he began, not quite understanding.

"My publisher has always said that even though I'm using a man's name, readers—the real die-hard mystery fans, anyway—would be able to tell."

"That the author's really a woman?"

She nodded.

"I seriously doubt it.

"Whatever made you decide to write this kind of book?" Brian asked, his interest apparently genuine.

"Simple. I wanted to write the kind of book I like

to read.'' She turned to look at him momentarily. ''Apparently, Mr. Reynolds—''

''Brian,'' he corrected.

''Brian.'' She turned her focus back to the road. ''Apparently, we have something in common.''

He suddenly seemed uncomfortable. ''So it would seem.''

John spoke up then. ''Not a bad start,'' he quipped. ''Dad...''

''She's pretty, isn't she?''

''Dad!''

Amy laughed. She could see why her mother had loved him so much.

She could also see why Brian was so frustrated.

His father continued to fire questions at Amy, questions about her mother. Neither of them noticed that he had withdrawn from the conversation about twenty minutes ago, disinterested, not really even wanting to listen to what they were saying. Staring through the window at the mostly rural scenery rolling past him, he nodded off before he even realized he was doing so....

New York City. Brian and Amy were together on the observation deck at the top of the Empire State Building. They were dressed in clothes from the early 1940s—Amy wore a bright yellow silk scarf around her neck. The wind was blowing, but neither of them seemed to care.

"I don't want to go home tomorrow," she told him.

"I don't want you to go." He held her close. "But I don't think we have a choice."

She sighed heavily. "No, Daddy made it quite clear that staying on is out of the question."

"I wish there were some way we could have more time together," he said wistfully. "It won't be long before I'll have to enlist—"

"America isn't at war!"

"Not yet, but we will be—probably very soon," he predicted. "No point in waiting until the last minute to sign up."

"Do you have to?"

"I think I should, don't you?"

"You're right, of course." She looked a little embarrassed. "I just hate the idea of us being so far apart so soon after finding each other."

"I'm not crazy about the idea, either," he told her, "but maybe it won't be for all that long."

"I hope not."

At that moment, an unexpected strong gust of wind swept across the observation deck, whipping the scarf from around her neck.

"My scarf!" she cried.

They both ran after it, but before either of them could get close enough to grab it, another gust of wind swept it upward and over the fence that surrounded the observation deck.

"Oh, no!"

He took her in his arms and kissed away her tears—

It was at that moment that Brian woke up.

What a corny dream, he thought.

"Pats, we're here!"

Amy called out to her sister as she entered the house, something she'd always done, even as a child. Brian and John coming in behind her were silent, waiting for a response.

Patti appeared at the top of the stairs. "You bellowed?"

"I didn't wake up Mom, did I?"

"You woke up the whole neighborhood," Patti told her. "But as for Mom, she was already awake when your ship sailed into port."

"Great!" Amy waved her hand expansively. "My sister, Patti. Pats, this is John Reynolds and his son, Brian."

Patti came down the stairs to greet them properly. "I'm so pleased to meet both of you," she said, smiling as she shook hands with them.

Brian was amazed. These two women seemed not only pleased to be reuniting their mother with her long-lost love, but downright thrilled. Why? he wondered. Didn't they care about their father? Wasn't he a good father, a good husband?

Amy and Patti seemed to think reuniting their mother and his father was the most wonderful thing in the world. How could they think it was wonderful? Hadn't their mother been carrying a torch all these years, as his father had? Hadn't their childhood been as miserable as his?

He couldn't remember if Amy had ever mentioned the situation between her parents, the state of their marriage. He didn't think so. She had said her father was deceased, that she hadn't known about her mother's romance with his father until after her own father's death.

Maybe her childhood wasn't so bad, he thought. Maybe her parents didn't fight all the time. Maybe they had had a good marriage.

Maybe Marian only looked up my father now because she's lonely since her husband passed away.

"Brian?"

His head jerked up. "What?"

Patti touched his arm. "Amy's taking your father upstairs to see Mom," she said. "Are you coming?"

He nodded and headed for the stairs. He wasn't at all sure how he felt about being present when his father came face-to-face again with the woman who'd always been a wedge between his parents, but he'd come this far—he couldn't very well refuse now.

"I'm coming."

He brought up the rear as they headed upstairs. Amy led the way to her mother's room, grinning broadly as she opened the door.

"Hi, Mom!" she greeted. "Look who I found!"

Her mother's eyes widened. "John?" she asked. "John Reynolds, is that really you?"

"There can't be two of us!" He ran to her side. "Marian, I still can't believe it. I never thought I'd ever see you again!"

"I wasn't even sure you were still alive," she told him.

Brian wished he hadn't come.

They still love each other, Amy decided.

Watching her mother and John together, seeing each other again for the first time in over fifty years, that one single fact was undeniable.

They were still very much in love.

She couldn't help but wonder what might have happened if they had been reunited sooner—perhaps when her father was still alive.

How would you have felt then, Mom? she wondered. *What would you have done?*

Would you have stayed with Dad, or would you have left him for John?

Amy was beginning to understand how Brian felt, how he'd felt most of his life. Had that happened, had her mother left her father for this man she'd loved for so long, Amy was certain she would have felt every bit as bitter toward John as Brian did toward her mother. And then some.

They still love each other, Brian decided.

Seeing them together, he knew his mother had been

right. His father had never loved his mother. It was always Marian—it always had been, as far as his father was concerned.

Even now, after all these years, it's still there, he thought.

They're still in love.

What must it be like to love someone that much? he wondered. What must it be like to grow up surrounded by that kind of love?

He wished he knew.

He wished his mother could have known.

5

"You've never married?" Amy asked as they sat on the front porch, drinking tea while Patti made dinner.

Brian shook his head. "Once, but my wife died," he admitted.

Amy wanted to ask more but figured it was none of her business, so she kept quiet and hoped he would volunteer an explanation.

He did. "I was afraid after Elaine died," he told her. "She was special. I figured that type of feeling only comes around once in a lifetime. And I certainly didn't want to end up like my parents."

"It was that bad—between your parents, I mean?"

He nodded. "When I was young, it wasn't all that bad," he recalled, "but I can't remember it ever being a warm, loving relationship."

"They must have loved each other once," Amy concluded, "or they wouldn't have married in the first place."

"Oh, my mother loved my father," Brian said.

"No doubt about that. She loved him too much, actually."

"Too much?" It made Amy think of her own failed marriage to Parker.

"It was too much considering the kind of marriage she'd made for herself." There was sadness in his voice. "My mother married my father knowing he was still in love with your mother, knowing he'd never really gotten over her."

"He told her that?" Amy asked, surprised.

"He didn't have to," Brian said. "Burke's Harbor was an even smaller town than it is now. There were no secrets."

"It must have been difficult for her to take a chance on making him love her." Amy couldn't begin to imagine marrying under such circumstances.

"She told me she'd been in love with him since they were kids," he said. "She always thought they'd get married."

"Then he went to New York and met my mother."

Brian nodded. "He came back to Burke's Harbor and broke it off with my mother."

"Mom said they saw each other every chance they got," Amy recalled. "She told me she was scared to death when he went off to war."

"So was my mother."

"Mom was sure they'd get married after the war," Amy said. "She talked about how much they loved each other, how they wrote as often as they could."

"Until the last letter was lost," Brian said.

Amy nodded. "When your father's letters stopped coming, my mother thought he was either dead or had met someone else," she said. "It broke her heart."

"If she thought he was dead, why didn't she try to contact his family?" Brian asked.

"I don't know," Amy replied. "Maybe she just didn't want to know, either way. She's never talked much about it."

"Dad talked to Katie about it after Mom left," Brian said. "But not to me. Never to me."

"He must have known how you felt about it."

"I never made any secret of it," Brian said truthfully.

"What sort of things did he tell Katie?" Amy hoped he knew.

"He said he'd wanted to marry Marian," said Brian. "He said he'd planned to marry her after the war, when he came back to the States."

"Obviously, he did," Amy said, thinking of the letter.

Brian nodded. "When she didn't reply to his proposal, it hurt him deeply," he said, remembering what Katie had told him. "He thought she'd changed her mind, that she just didn't want to marry him."

"He never tried to find her, either."

"Nope." He paused. "I wonder what things would be like today if that letter had been delivered on time?"

"We wouldn't be here, for one thing," she stated.

He looked at her, surprised. "Huh?"

"Think about it," she told him. "Your father and my mother would be celebrating their golden wedding anniversary by now," she said. "My father and your mother would have married others. They all probably would have had children—but those children would not have been us."

"How do you figure?"

"Different genetic makeup."

He nodded. "I suppose you're right."

"Scary, isn't it?"

"The idea that we were only born because of a mistake?" he asked. "I'll say."

"Does that make me selfish?"

"What?"

"Being glad my parents did get together. Being glad to be alive."

"If it does, it puts me in the same boat," he confessed.

"Do you ever think about what might have been— for us, I mean?" Marian asked.

John gave her a tired smile. They sat on the porch swing, watching the sunset. "Not a day has passed in fifty years that I haven't thought about it," he assured her.

She touched his face gently. "Weren't you happy, John?" she asked.

"Not the way I would have been with you," he said honestly.

"I'm sorry."

"It wasn't your fault," John insisted.

"If I had known—"

"If *I* had known, I would've written again," he told her. "I would've kept writing until I got an answer."

"What about Rhonda?" Marian asked. "Didn't you love her at all?"

He frowned. "In my own way, I loved her," he said quietly. "I loved her more than she thought I did, a lot more than she thought I did."

"But?" Marian knew there was something he wasn't saying.

"But she wasn't you," he said. "I was never able to love her the way I loved you."

"Did you give her a chance?"

"Yes, I did," he insisted. "I tried every way I could to make that marriage work! She knew, though."

"Knew what?"

"That I'd never been able to stop loving you," he said. "Oh, I wanted to. I really tried. I didn't want to go on hurting like that."

She put her hand on his. "That was the last thing I wanted to do, John—hurt you, I mean."

"I know that now," he said. "But back then, all I

could do was wonder why you'd suddenly changed your mind about me, about us.''

Marian smiled patiently. "It would seem that we both jumped to the same conclusion,'' she said.

His eyes met hers. "I've missed you, Marian.''

"I've missed you, too, John.''

"What do you think they're talking about?'' Brian wondered out loud.

"Old times?'' Amy guessed.

"They really did love each other, didn't they?''

Amy smiled. "They really do,'' she corrected. Looking through the living room window at them now, there wasn't the slightest doubt in her mind.

"Think they'll get back together now, after all these years?''

"I'd bet on it.'' Amy looked at him, suddenly concerned. "How will you feel about it if they do?''

He thought about it. "I don't know,'' he said truthfully.

"Think you can handle it?''

"I don't think I'll have a choice, do you?'' he asked. "It's his life. It's his decision.''

"But how will you handle it?'' she persisted.

"I guess I'll just have to accept it, won't I?'' He was still watching them through the front window.

"That's comforting,'' Amy said in a dull tone.

"It's nothing against your mother...'' he began.

"Sure it is!'' she retorted. "You've admitted to

having spent most of your life hating my mother for coming between your mother and father.''

"I was a kid from a broken home," he reminded her. "How was I supposed to feel?"

Amy nodded. "I guess I would have felt the same way if—"

"If your parents had divorced," he finished the sentence for her.

"Yeah," she said quietly.

"But they didn't, did they?"

She shook her head. "No," she said, "they didn't."

"Let me guess," he began. "You had a nice, normal, typically middle-class family life with two parents who had a great relationship. You and your sister were best friends. You had a dog, a station wagon, the whole nine yards."

"Close," she admitted.

"You didn't even know about *my* father until after *your* father died."

"No. I didn't."

"If my life had been like that when I was growing up, I wouldn't have been bitter, either," he told her. "What I grew up with wasn't such a pretty picture. My parents fought a lot—screaming was the normal tone of voice used around our house. The best we could hope for was an armed truce. I spent my nights, more often than not, with the pillow over my head instead of under it so I could muffle the sounds of them yelling at each other.''

"I'm sorry,'' Amy said, and she meant it. It must have been tough, she thought.

"So was I.''

"How old were you when they divorced?'' she asked, not sure she really should.

He shrugged. "About ten, eleven,'' he said, feigning indifference. "The day they threw in the towel was like the end of the world for me. I wanted to die, I really did.''

"I can imagine.'' Amy was thinking of her own divorce.

"Can you?'' He looked dubious.

She nodded. "More than you know.''

"How? You had the picture-perfect family—''

"It's a long story.''

He said nothing, waiting for her to continue.

"Some other time,'' she said, making it clear that she wasn't about to discuss it further.

"He's a tough nut to crack, that's for sure,'' Patti commented.

Through the living room window, Amy could see Brian's taxi pulling away. "He's got years of bitterness to deal with,'' she said quietly. She wished he hadn't been so insistent upon leaving now, instead of waiting for his father.

"How so?''

"His parents divorced years ago," Amy said. "Apparently it was never a very happy marriage."

"And he blames our mother for that?" Patti protested. "That's why he won't stay?"

"He believes that things would have been different if his father hadn't been in love with our mother all these years," Amy explained.

"Sure."

"It's true," Amy insisted.

Patti shrugged. "I suppose he needs to blame somebody."

"He told me his mother had been in love with his father since they were kids," Amy remembered. "He said she had every reason to expect that they would be married."

"And then John met Mom," Patti concluded.

Amy nodded.

"And he dropped Rhonda?"

Amy nodded again.

"But they did get back together—obviously," Patti reminded her.

"They did, eventually," said Amy. "But only after he went off to war, after he wrote to Mom, asking her to be his wife and never got an answer."

"He married her on the rebound."

"Something like that, yes."

Patti frowned. "Not the best reason to get married."

Amy shook her head. "In their case, it turned out

to be the worst possible reason," she said. "According to Brian, they were never happy."

"I can imagine."

"Katie, Brian's sister, apparently handled it all pretty well," Amy told Patti. "Brian, on the other hand, grew up cynical and resentful. He allowed himself to get close to one woman and she died. He's never allowed himself to get into an intimate relationship with a woman since."

"He told you this?"

Amy paused. "Yes."

Patti nodded. "It would seem the two of you have a lot in common, then," she commented.

Amy looked at her, surprised. "How do you figure?"

"Oh, come on—don't play dumb with me," Patti admonished. "You've been wary of men ever since you and Parker split up."

"Not to the extent that Brian is with women," Amy protested.

"No?" Patti looked unconvinced.

"No!"

"Then tell me—why is it you haven't dated, not even once, since Parker left?" Patti asked smugly.

Amy gave her an offhanded shrug. "I haven't met anyone I've wanted to go out with, that's all."

"You'll excuse me if I don't believe that," Patti responded dubiously.

"I don't care if you do or not," Amy said defensively. "I don't even want to talk about this."

"You *need* to talk about it," Patti persisted. "You *need* to deal with your feelings before you end up like Brian Reynolds—alone and unhappy."

Amy said nothing, but figured it was probably already too late. Was that why she had such strong—and ambivalent—feelings toward him? There was a common bond between them—both had been hurt, both were wary of relationships—that at once drew them together and pulled them apart.

Brian counted maybe half a dozen people in his car on the late afternoon train. He was grateful for the absence of a crowd, grateful for the solitude.

He needed to think.

At the moment, sorting out his feelings was no small feat. Some of them, many of them, maybe most of them, couldn't be easily identified.

It was hard not to be moved by the enduring love shared by his father and Marian Haskell Barrington. Seeing them together made it clear that their love was rare indeed.

It was also painfully obvious that John Reynolds had never loved his ex-wife that way and never could. It was a reminder of all of the pain of his childhood.

And then there was Amy.

How did he feel about her? Did he feel anything for her? He wasn't sure if he did or not. His emotions seemed to all be tied up with his ambivalent feelings toward her mother.

It wasn't fair to Amy, he knew that. It wasn't her fault, any more than it was his, but he couldn't help how he felt. He looked at Amy and saw her mother, saw the woman who'd always stood between his parents. He saw the reason for his lifelong unhappiness. Irrational though that might be, it was just how he felt.

He asked himself how he'd feel about her if they'd met under different circumstances. If she hadn't been Marian's daughter, but he had no answer...because there was no way he could separate Amy from her mother.

Amy was an attractive woman. Not his type— whatever his type was, these days he wasn't quite sure—but very attractive.

But that's as far as it goes, he told himself.

Yeah, he's good-looking, Amy's conscience muttered. *So what?*

Amy was still thinking about her conversation with Patti about Brian. Her attitude toward marriage was hardly the same as Brian's.

She'd been married. She'd been betrayed by a man she'd loved and trusted. A man she'd once believed loved her.

Of course she was gun-shy.

But Brian Reynolds had been married once before,

to a woman he loved, a woman who died, according to his sister. Coming from a broken home wasn't exactly the same thing.

Was it?

She didn't have a clue. Not having come from a divorced family herself, she couldn't even imagine what growing up must have been like for Brian and Katie. She couldn't imagine what it would have been like to grow up without either of her parents.

It could have happened, though, she reminded herself. It could have happened if Mom and John had been reunited sooner.

If her mother had received John's letter sooner.

"Want to talk about it?" Katie asked, stopping at the porch steps to her father's house.

Brian sat on the front porch, alone in the darkness until her arrival, lost in thought. "He stayed in Boston," he said quietly.

Katie climbed the few steps and moved to sit down beside him. "Does that surprise you?"

"No," he admitted, shaking his head. "I'd hoped he wouldn't, though."

"He's waited a long time for this."

Brian nodded. "I know."

"You still haven't let him go, have you?" she asked.

He turned to look at her for the first time. "What are you talking about?"

"You know what I'm talking about," Katie maintained.

"Katie—"

"Mom and Dad just didn't belong together, Bri," she said. "They're better off apart."

"They could have worked things out if—"

Katie shook her head. "We don't know that."

"I do."

"No, you don't."

"You never did care, did you?"

She recoiled as if he'd physically struck her. "That's not true!"

"You sure never showed it," he responded sharply.

"That doesn't mean I didn't care," she said, defending herself. "I didn't want to see them split up, either—but they just weren't happy, Brian. They never would have been."

"They didn't have a chance," he said stubbornly.

"They had thirty years of opportunities," Katie argued. "They couldn't make it work."

"Mom loved him."

"But he didn't love her," Katie reminded him.

"He never tried."

"Love isn't something that can be forced," she said.

"I'm not so sure it even exists," he said coldly.

"That's why you're miserable and alone now," she said accusingly. "If you ever decide to let go of all of that anger and bitterness, you just might find someone and be happy yourself.''

''Has it ever occurred to you that maybe I don't want to?''

''Don't want to what?'' she asked. ''Find someone? Or be happy?''

''Both.'' He stood. ''I'm going down to the boathouse. Do me a big favor and don't follow me.''

''I think maybe you've had a little too much excitement for one day, Mom,'' Amy worried aloud as she and Patti helped Marian into bed.

''Nonsense,'' Marian huffed, leaning forward to allow Patti to adjust her pillows. ''This is the very best medicine you could have given me.''

Over the top of Marian's head, Patti gave Amy the evil eye. ''That remains to be seen,'' she said tightly.

''Seeing John has been a dream come true,'' Marian continued. ''I didn't think I would ever see him again, ever know what became of him.''

''I'm happy for you, Mom,'' Amy told her, ''but we can't have you overdoing it, now.''

''Overdoing it!'' Marian snorted. ''I haven't seen John in over fifty years!''

''Exactly,'' Patti said. ''You tried to cram fifty years of catching up into a few hours. It's not like you're never going to see him again.''

''That's what I thought when he went off to war

in 1942,'' Marian argued. "And look how long I had to wait!"

"This time you won't have to wait that long," Amy promised. "He'll still be here when you wake up."

"He's staying?" Marian asked hopefully.

"For another day, anyway."

Marian nodded, settling back against the pillows. "Don't let me sleep too long, all right?"

"We won't," Amy assured her.

She followed Patti out of the room and closed the door. "It's been quite a day, hasn't it?" she commented.

"I'm not sure this was such a good idea," Patti told her.

"How can you say that?" Amy asked. "Look at her!"

"I am looking at her." Patti tried to keep her voice down. "That's why I don't think it was a good idea."

"She's happier than she's been since Dad died," Amy reminded her.

"She's also totally exhausted," her sister observed pointedly. "You know as well as I do—maybe better—how her doctors feel about letting her overdo it."

"She loves this man!" Amy said with conviction. "How can that be anything but right?"

6

Brian was glad to be home.

And he was glad Amy was still in Boston.

Ever since her arrival in Burke's Harbor, his life had been in a constant state of chaos. The quiet calm of his familiar laid-back, small-town life had been shaken to its foundations by her sudden intrusion.

He'd finally accepted his father's past, even if he'd never been able to understand it. But now...

Now, because of *her,* because of Amy, the past was no longer just a phantom, a ghost of his father's dreams. Marian Haskell was a real, flesh-and-blood woman; a woman his father still loved deeply.

And her daughter was a flesh-and-blood woman, as well.

"I can't thank you enough for coming to see my mother," Amy told John when they were on the road, headed back to Burke's Harbor. "It meant so much to her—"

"No more than it's meant to me," he assured her. "I never thought I'd ever see her again."

"She felt pretty much the same way," Amy said, keeping her eyes on the road as they followed the coast north. They were expected at Katie's by late afternoon. "I think this was absolutely the best thing that could have happened to her."

"But?" he asked. "I get the feeling there's more."

She nodded. "I'm worried about her," she admitted. "As you know, she recently had major surgery. It was a tumor. Benign, but it was frightening for all of us. She's not a young woman anymore."

"You think this was too much for her?" he asked, suddenly concerned.

"I think she overdid it," Amy said honestly, "but with rest, she'll bounce back, I'm sure."

"She always was strong," John recalled. "One of the many things I always loved about her."

"What was she like back then?" Amy really wanted to know.

"Oh, she was something!" The memory made him smile. "A real spitfire—full of spirit."

"Mom?"

"Hard for you to believe, is it?"

"Well...yes."

"I can't imagine the years could have changed her all that much." He paused thoughtfully. "When we met, she was sixteen. I was eighteen. We hadn't gotten into the war yet, but it was already in full swing in Europe.''

''That was the summer she stayed with her aunt Bessie?''

He nodded. ''I was staying with family, too. We met on the escalator at Macy's department store,'' he said.

Amy chuckled. ''She never told me that. An escalator?''

''Yep. We were stuck between a lady with four screaming kids and a guy who looked for all the world like Alfred Hitchcock.''

The image that conjured up in Amy's mind made her laugh. ''Must have been pleasant,'' she commented.

''It was,'' he said truthfully. ''Once I met Marian, I didn't notice much of anything else.''

''Love at first sight?''

He shook his head. ''I don't really believe in that,'' he said, ''but there was something there. Something definitely clicked between us.''

''Obviously.''

''We were together almost constantly from that day on,'' he continued. ''At least as much as our families would permit.''

Amy nodded. ''She told me.''

''She talked to you about us? That surprises me,'' he said.

"She talked about you a lot after Dad died," Amy told him.

"Was she happy with him—your father, I mean?"

Amy couldn't decide if he hoped she would say yes—or not. "They always seemed to be happy," she said truthfully.

"I'm glad," he said, nodding. "No matter what, I always hoped wherever she was, she was happy."

"She wished the same for you."

John frowned. "I didn't fare as well as she did."

"I know."

"Brian told you?"

Amy frowned. "In no uncertain terms."

John apologized for his son's actions. "Brian's bitter. Always has been," he said regretfully. "I guess he has a right to be, though."

"Why do you say that?"

"Couldn't have been easy for him," John said, shaking his head. "Growing up the way he did, with his mother and me fighting most of the time."

"I don't know," Amy began. "It doesn't seem to have had much of an effect on Katie."

He nodded. "Different kids handle things differently, I guess," he said. "Katie always was pretty resilient."

"But Brian wasn't?"

"Brian was a sensitive kid," John said. "Everything affected him."

"I think it still does."

"The two of you don't get along very well, do you?"

"Sometimes we do, sometimes we don't," she said, wishing, as she had right from the beginning, that she understood Brian Reynolds—but then, she wondered if he even understood himself.

"That pretty much describes Brian's relationships in general," John told her.

"That bad?"

"That bad."

"He's never been able to trust a woman?" Amy was surprised.

"Worse. He's never been able to trust himself," John revealed.

"Himself?"

"He feels things deeply," John explained. "Those feelings scare the daylights out of him, so he keeps a tight rein on them."

"Why do they scare him?"

"He grew up seeing his mother's pain, believing emotions not controlled brought nothing but pain," he recalled. "He won't let himself love anybody."

I know the feeling, Amy thought.

"If you're so worried about him being in Boston, why did you leave him there?" Katie asked Brian. They sat in the kitchen of the B and B, awaiting Amy and John's arrival.

"What was I supposed to do?" he asked irritably.

"He was determined to stay—I couldn't very well hog-tie him and drag him back here."

"Frankly, I don't understand why you're so upset about him being there in the first place," Katie told him. "He and Mom have been divorced a long time now. There's no reason why he shouldn't move on with his life."

"Mom hasn't."

"That's her choice."

"No, Katie, it isn't her choice," Brian argued. "She doesn't like any of this."

"She didn't want the divorce, no," Katie agreed. "But she's made no attempt to get on with her own life since the divorce."

"She doesn't want a life of her own," Brian said tightly.

"What she wants, she can't have, Bri," Katie reminded him. "She's going to have to accept that, sooner or later."

"She can't."

"So, Dad's supposed to live the life of a recluse, too—is that it?" Katie asked.

"Tell me something, did he ever care about her at all?" There was unmasked bitterness in his voice.

"Oh, Brian, I'm sure he always has—"

"He has a funny way of showing it!" Brian snapped. "He's never brought her anything but misery for as long as I can remember." His face was dark with rage.

"He cared. I'm sure he did," Katie insisted. "He just never was able to love her in the same way that she loved him."

"He shouldn't have married her, then."

"Probably not," she conceded, "but he did."

"Why?" Brian wondered out loud.

"Maybe he thought he'd come to love her—who knows? Why did you marry Elaine?" Katie shrugged.

"I don't know. I loved her, I guess, but we're talking about Dad here. He thought he was just settling for second best," Brian presumed.

"Brian, that's just not true!" Katie stared at him for a moment. "When are you ever going to let go of all that anger?" she asked finally.

"I don't know," he answered truthfully. "Maybe never, I just don't know."

"I hope you do...for your sake," she told him. "I'd hate to think you'd be this miserable for the rest of your life."

"Who said I'm miserable?"

"Unfortunately, nobody has to say it," she responded. "It's so obvious. You wear it like a neon sign."

"Listen, sis. I'm alone because I *want* to be alone," he told her. "I like things the way they are."

"Sure you do."

"I do," he insisted. "I think I'm probably better off, in fact."

"Better off than who?"

"Better off than all of you fools who wear your hearts on your sleeves and invariably end up getting them bruised and battered," he said.

"It's a risk worth taking," Katie maintained.

"Is it?" he asked dubiously.

"Yes, Brian, it is! You and Elaine had a wonderful marriage. As for me, Jerry and the kids are the best thing that's ever happened to me," she said. "I knew when I met him that things might not turn out the way I wanted them to between us, that I could end up with a broken heart—but I took that chance, and I thank my lucky stars every day that I did."

"But then, you didn't marry a man who was in love with someone else," he reminded her.

"And you don't have to marry a woman who's still in love with someone else!" she flung back at him stubbornly.

"I don't have to marry anybody!"

"No, you don't—you can go right on feeling sorry for yourself and being miserable and alone," she said, exasperated.

"You live your life, and I'll live mine, okay?" He walked out, slamming the door in his wake.

"Where's your brother?" Amy asked Katie.

"Down at the docks. Some man called this morning about chartering a boat." Katie watched her father as he climbed the stairs to freshen up before Katie drove him home.

"He didn't want to be here when we came back," Amy guessed.

"He didn't say that, no."

"Maybe not, but I'd be willing to bet money that it was what he was thinking," Amy said with certainty.

"I don't know."

But Amy had a feeling she really did. It's hard to believe those two are brother and sister, she thought. She's so open, so friendly, and he's so uptight and bad-tempered.

"How did it go?" Katie finally asked.

Amy smiled. "Like the climax of an old movie," she said with a sigh. "I almost started believing in fairy tales again, watching them together."

"Think they'll see each other again?" Katie inquired.

"I'm sure of it."

"I'm happy for them," Katie said. "Dad's been alone a long time now—too long, really. He needs someone in his life, someone he cares for."

Amy gave her a halfhearted smile. "I'm not sure your brother would share that sentiment," she said wearily.

"My brother's got a lot of emotional baggage to deal with," Katie said quietly.

"Obviously."

"I wish he'd date again."

Katie's statement took Amy by surprise. "Think

that would help?'' she asked, trying not to laugh, re-
alizing how serious Katie was.

''I don't know,'' Katie said, ''but I have to wonder
if Brian's biggest problem doesn't stem from the fact
that he's never been in love himself.''

''How do you figure?''

''He doesn't know what it's like, so he can't em-
pathize with what Dad's feeling.''

''Probably not,'' Amy agreed with a nod.

''He doesn't know what he's missing.''

Sometimes I wonder, Amy thought. Sometimes I
think maybe we'd all be better off if we did miss that
particular experience.

Out loud she said, ''With his attitude, I doubt he'll
ever have that experience.''

''Unfortunately, you're right.''

''Seems like a rather severe overreaction to your
parents' divorce,'' Amy said thoughtfully.

Katie nodded. ''He and Mom are very close—always were,'' she stated. ''He was protective of her,
even as a little boy. When she and Dad argued, she'd
lock herself in the bedroom and cry. Brian would stuff
tissues under the door to her and beg her to stop.''

''Being that close, I'm surprised he's not especially
sensitive to women,'' Amy said.

Katie sighed heavily. ''He's always said he'd never
marry again because he didn't want to put a woman
through what our mother went through—as he put
it.''

Just as I said I'd never marry again because I didn't want to go through what Parker put me through again, Amy was thinking.

"I thought I'd find you here."

Brian looked up as Amy walked down the dock toward him. "What are you doing here?" he asked, his tone indifferent.

"Looking for you, obviously."

"I can see that," he said, going on about his business as if she weren't there, "but why are you looking for me?"

"I thought you'd want to know that we'd arrived." She sat down on the edge of the dock, letting her bare legs dangle.

She *did* look good in shorts, he thought, mentally cursing himself for even noticing. "I assumed you would," he said, wishing she'd just go away.

"Don't you want to know how it went?" she asked, staring out over the water.

"I think I can guess."

Amy was silent for a long moment. "You don't want our parents to rediscover each other, do you?"

"He's a grown man. That's his business," he said tightly.

"I know that," Amy said, turning her head to look at him. "But that's not what I asked you."

"It doesn't matter what I think."

"It does to me."

"Why?"

"Because if they do get together, you'll be her stepson. I don't want my mother to get hurt," she answered truthfully.

"You have nothing to worry about," he assured Amy, rising to put himself at eye level with her. "If they get married, they probably won't see me more than once a year."

Her eyes narrowed. "Your attitude stinks, Reynolds," she told him.

"Why? Because I don't relish the idea of spending time with my father and his potential new wife?" He glared at her. "I'm a grown man, and I'm entitled to the way I feel—that's my right."

"Sometimes I wonder."

"I beg your pardon?"

"Sometimes I wonder..." she repeated, "about whether you really are a grown man or not. Sometimes you just act like some spoiled brat!"

"Do you think I really care what you think of me?" he asked, angry that she had the nerve to judge him.

"No—that's the problem," she snapped irritably. "I don't think you care what anyone thinks. I don't think you care about anyone."

"Not that I need to explain myself to you," he began, biting off each word as if it had an excruciatingly bitter taste, "but there are some people I do care very deeply about.'' He started to move away from her.

''But not your father.''

''Did I say that?''

''You didn't have to.''

He turned on her angrily. ''Why did you have to come here, anyway?'' he demanded hotly. ''We were doing fine until you showed up and reopened all the old wounds!''

''Were you?'' She was dubious.

What happened next made no sense at all, even to him. He acted without thinking, grabbing her shoulders and pulling her off the dock toward him. He kissed her, deeply but not roughly, with a passion that left him just as speechless as she was.

7

Brian looked embarrassed; Amy, for the first time in her life, was speechless.

"What was that all about?" she finally managed to ask.

"A mistake," he said, avoiding her eyes. "It was a mistake."

"Why, then?"

"Why did I do it?"

"Seems like a valid question."

Still, they avoided any eye contact.

"I don't know why I did it," he answered nervously.

She wasn't buying it. "You must have some idea," she persisted.

"I don't."

"You don't have a clue, or you don't intend to tell me?"

He moved to the back of the boat he'd been working on when she'd arrived, still not looking at her. "Let me put it this way— if I *did* know, I wouldn't tell you," he said tightly. "Now, I have work to do, so will you please just go away?"

"Now that's the kind of sweet talk a girl likes to hear," Amy said, hiding her nervousness as she always did, behind a lot of false bravado.

He ignored her, focusing all of his attention on the boat. Finally, Amy gave up. "Okay, have it your way, honey," she said, forcing a lightness into her voice that she didn't really feel. "I'll be going now."

He didn't respond.

She scrambled out of the boat and headed up the dock, vowing not to look back. Yet she couldn't help herself. She broke that vow before she reached the end.

What is it with him, anyway? she wondered, watching Brian do his level best to ignore her. What's his problem?

When Amy first came to Burke's Harbor, Brian had acted as if she'd had cooties or something. He hadn't been even remotely friendly until the drive to Boston. Then he seemed to warm up to her a little. Now he was as cold as ice.

What happened?

She went back to the bed and breakfast, where she found Katie in the kitchen. "Sometimes, it seems totally impossible that the two of you could be related," Amy announced, irritated.

"I take it the other half of the two of us you're

referring to is my brother,'' Katie said with a knowing smile.

"Who else?" Amy rolled her eyes skyward.

"What's he done now?"

Amy sighed heavily. "He kissed me."

Katie stopped what she was doing, stunned. "He—what?"

"He kissed me."

"Why?"

"I don't have a clue."

Katie looked puzzled. "Wait a minute," she said. "There was nothing going on between you—"

"We were arguing," Amy recalled.

"Arguing?" Now Katie was really confused.

"Arguing," Amy said, nodding. "It came right out of the blue, totally unexpected."

Katie thought about it for a moment. "This is strange, even for Brian," she admitted.

Amy grinned. "You took the words right out of my mouth."

"Unless..."

"Unless what?"

"Maybe he has feelings for you he's trying to hide," Katie suggested.

"You mean, the homicidal type," Amy concluded.

"No, I mean the romantic type."

"Oh, please!"

"I'm serious," Katie insisted. "My brother was so devastated by our parents' divorce and then Elaine's death, he swore he'd never let himself fall in love again."

"He's got a great technique for driving women away," Amy offered as a testimonial to his determination.

"He didn't want to end up in the kind of painful relationship our mother had," Katie explained. "Our mother wasn't happy and she wasn't at all good at hiding it," Katie said, slicing a tomato carefully. "Brian and Mom were so close, her pain became his pain."

"I'm sorry." Amy really meant it.

"From what you've told me," Katie went on, "he did what he did on the spur of the moment. On impulse. He let his feelings show before he could censor them."

"I thought he was trying to drive me away," Amy told her. "Which he didn't have to do, since I wasn't planning to stay anyway."

Katie looked surprised. "You're leaving?" she asked.

Amy nodded. "I've done what I came here to do," she said. "There's no reason to stick around."

"Isn't there?"

Amy gave her a quizzical look.

"How do you feel about my brother, Amy?" Katie asked.

"What kind of a question is that?" Amy asked defensively.

"An honest one, I think."

"We haven't exactly been Romeo and Juliet," she said sarcastically.

"That doesn't answer my question."

"I haven't given it much thought, one way or the other," Amy lied, thinking of the dream she'd had about him when she first came to Burke's Harbor.

"Are you sure about that?"

"What makes you think I have?"

Katie shrugged. "I don't know. I can't explain it," she admitted. "It's just a feeling I have."

Amy responded with a laugh she didn't really feel. "Better get your radar checked, Katie," she advised. "It's way out of whack."

Stupid, stupid, stupid!

Brian reprimanded himself all the way home. *How could I have been so stupid?*

Kissing Amy Barrington was, without a doubt, the dumbest thing he'd ever done.

So why had he done it?

He wished he knew, he thought miserably. Fishing his keys from the pocket of his jeans, he unlocked the front door and let himself into the house.

"Dad?" he called.

No answer.

He's probably over at the veterans' hall, sharing his wonderful news with all of his old buddies, Brian thought. Reunited with the love of his life.

If I were a good son, I'd be happy for him. Wouldn't I?

Then he noticed the shoe box on the couch, the box of old letters his father had brought down from the attic the night before they'd left for Boston. Letters from Marian Haskell. Letters his father had wanted him to read.

Dad thought reading them would help him understand, he recalled, still staring at the box. But how could a bunch of letters erase the pain of a lifetime?

He flopped down onto the couch, rubbing his temples. He had one monumental headache. The incident with Amy at the dock had thrown him for a loop. He'd done something he hadn't expected to do, hadn't wanted to do.

So why did I do it?

Willing to do just about anything to get his mind off Amy Barrington and that kiss, he looked down at the box of letters again. *He asked me to read them,* he thought. *I guess I wouldn't be invading his privacy if I read them now.*

He picked up one of the envelopes and opened it. The letter was dated May, 1943.

"Dear John..." Brian smiled to himself. A Dear John letter?

Get serious, Reynolds!

Dear John,
I was in New York over the weekend. It reminded me of the last time we were there to-

gether. Remember when we went to the top of the Empire State Building? Remember how windy it was that day, how my scarf blew away? I hated to lose that beautiful yellow silk scarf because you gave it to me, but we did laugh, didn't we, as we watched the wind carry it out over Central Park!

I wish you were here now, my darling. I wish you were here with me, where I could be sure you were safe. I wish we could take a carriage ride in Central Park and go to the top of the Empire State Building and buy hot dogs from that vendor at Fifth Avenue and Central Park South.

Your photograph is on the table beside my bed where it's the first thing I see when I wake in the morning and the last thing I see when I go to bed at night. Not an hour passes that I don't think about you, that I don't wonder where you are and what you are doing.

I wish this horrible war was over!

All my love,
Marian

Brian frowned as he folded the letter and returned it to its envelope. It was a safe bet his father had never exchanged such letters with his mother during the war. He knew his mother had written to his father, but he also knew that his father had only written her a few times.

And Dad sure didn't keep any of her letters, Brian brooded silently.

Brian definitely has a problem. A big one.

Frustrated, Amy stuffed her clothes into her suitcase randomly, without bothering to fold anything.

I need this like I need a hole in my head!

This man doesn't know what he wants.

Or who, for that matter.

He kisses me, but says he's not attracted to me.

That makes sense...well, about as much sense as anything else he's said or done.

The question is, why am I so angry?

Patti would say I have feelings for this man.

Patti would be nuts.

She closed the suitcase, zipped it up, then realized she hadn't finished packing everything.

Maybe I do have a hole in my head.

What a stupid thing to do!

Brian still wasn't sure what had motivated him to do such a foolish thing.

He hadn't really wanted to kiss Amy Barrington.

Had he?

Katie would say that he had. Katie would probably tell him that, subconsciously, he had wanted to all along and had acted impulsively in a weak moment.

Sometimes, he thought, Katie read too much.

* * *

The more distance she could put between herself and this place, the better, Amy decided.

Brian Reynolds was a complication she didn't need in her life.

As if he was really in my life.

Or ever could be.

Catching sight of herself in the mirror, she paused to study her reflection for a moment.

She needed her head examined.

Why doesn't Amy just go home?

Why doesn't she just get out of my life so it can get back to normal? Brian wondered, thoroughly aggravated.

At least, what he knew as normal.

He hadn't been the happiest guy in the world, that was true, but compared to what he was feeling since meeting Amy his prior existence had been paradise.

Hadn't it?

Amy couldn't get away from Burke's Harbor fast enough.

She loaded her bags into the trunk of her car and drove off without looking back, without so much as a goodbye to anyone but Katie.

If she ever saw this place again, she told herself, it would be too soon.

* * *

Why does it bother me? Brian asked himself.

If I don't care, it shouldn't bother me, right?

But it did bother him.

Maybe he was only fooling himself.

If he was, however, he wasn't sure he wanted to know.

He wasn't sure at all.

Boy, was she way off base!

Amy was thinking about her conversation with Katie as she drove back to Boston. Katie had tried to convince her to stay, at least overnight if not longer, but Amy was anxious to get home.

More so than ever.

She told herself that what had happened at the dock shouldn't bother her. If she didn't care, it wouldn't bother her. At least, that's what Katie maintained.

Makes sense, her conscience confirmed.

The problem was, it did bother her. It bothered her a lot. But she still wasn't sure what bugged her most—Brian kissing her, or her reaction to it.

How do I feel about him, really?

She wished she knew.

She didn't know him well enough to wonder if she could be in love with him. She had a feeling no woman had ever known him that well—or ever would. He didn't want anyone to fall in love with him, didn't want to fall in love himself.

So why had he kissed her?

A very good question, but one Amy wasn't sure anyone could answer—except maybe Brian himself, and she wasn't one hundred percent sure about him.

He didn't appear to be in control of himself, actually. If he had been, she was certain he wouldn't have come within ten feet of her—unless, of course, he was forced to do so at gunpoint.

He definitely would not have kissed her even then. Would he?

She didn't have a clue as to what was going on in his head. He admitted to being ambivalent where his father and her mother were concerned. He'd been downright unfriendly toward her when they'd first met, when he'd found out who she was.

The sins of the mother.

Amy frowned. All her mother was guilty of was loving his father. He couldn't spend the rest of his life blaming her mother for the failure of his mother's marriage, could he?

On second thought, he probably could. No one else could, but Brian Reynolds could. He's an odd one, that's for sure.

Her stomach started to growl, and she suddenly remembered she hadn't eaten anything since breakfast—and she was ravenously hungry. She stopped at a coffee shop in a small town near the Massachusetts-New Hampshire state line.

Because it was late, the small eatery was all but

deserted. Amy took a booth near the windows and hoped with all her heart that the only waitress on duty wasn't asleep.

She certainly didn't appear to be moving, Amy thought, watching her intently, contemplating what she might do to the woman if she didn't wait on her pronto.

Finally the waitress looked up and saw her. In no great hurry, she came out from behind the counter and moved toward Amy's booth, unfriendly, unsmiling.

"We're out of just about everything." It sounded more like a warning than a statement. "It's almost closing time."

"That's all right, I'm not picky." Just desperate, she mused silently.

"That's good to hear."

"I thought it would be." Amy scanned the menu. "How about the hamburger—no, make that a cheeseburger."

"We're out of ground beef."

"I see. The tuna on toast?"

"No tuna."

Amy nodded. "A B.L.T.?"

"No bacon," they both said at the same time in exactly the same tone of voice.

"Let's make this a little easier, all right?" Amy asked wearily. "What *do* you have?"

"Some chili—not much, I don't think—and a couple of pieces of pie."

"What kind of pie?"

"Cherry and pecan."

"Fine. I'll take the chili and a piece of cherry pie."

Amy had her suspicions about the chili. It was no ordinary chili, she thought, eyeing the bowl set in front of her. Where did they get the ingredients—a toxic waste dump?

But she was hungry and ate it anyway. The pie was good, though.

Amy left and the waitress went to clear her table. She cursed loudly when she saw what Amy had left in lieu of a tip, scribbled on a folded paper napkin.

"A smile goes a long way."

8

"You read them?"

John looked down at the open box of letters next to Brian on the couch.

"You said you wanted me to."

His father nodded. "I did," he acknowledged. "Did you?"

"I read a couple of them, yeah."

"So, what did you think?" John asked, sitting opposite Brian in his favorite chair.

Brian frowned. "What was I supposed to think, Dad?" he asked, not completely sure what kind of response his father expected.

John sucked in his breath and ran his hand through his graying hair, a gesture of frustration. "I'd hoped that reading them would help you to understand."

"What I got from reading them, Dad," he began carefully, "is that you loved this woman and she loved you more than anything in this world."

He nodded.

"Dad, I've known that most of my life," he reminded him. "I've known it since I was old enough to understand why you and Mom were always fighting."

John studied him for a moment. "You're never going to forgive me for that, are you?" he asked finally.

"I didn't say that."

"You didn't have to."

Brian hesitated for a moment. "I can forgive, yes," he said quietly. "But I can't forget, Dad. Believe me, I've tried. I've really tried."

John was silent for a few moments. "Was your childhood that bad?"

"Didn't you think it was?" Brian wanted to know.

"I didn't enjoy fighting with your mother, if that's what you mean," John told him. "And in case you've forgotten, *I* didn't initiate those arguments, Brian. She did!"

"What did you expect?"

John gave him a puzzled look.

"She loved you, Dad. It tore her up that you never loved her."

"I married her."

"Do you really think that was enough for her?"

"It was enough for me," John said quietly. "It had to be."

"Had to be," Brian repeated slowly. "Had to be, because you thought the woman you really wanted was lost to you forever."

John didn't respond.

"That's it, isn't it?"

"I tried to give your mother a good life, Brian," John said in defense of himself. "I tried to be a good husband. After all, she did give me what mattered most to me—my kids."

"But you couldn't give her what she wanted most," Brian concluded.

"Brian—"

"She wanted your love, Dad."

John shook his head. "I tried."

"But you just couldn't love her."

"In my own way, I did."

"Just not enough."

John hesitated, but only for a moment. "Tell me something, son..." He paused. "Do you intend to spend the rest of your life alone because you're afraid of ending up like your mother and me?"

Brian frowned. "It's crossed my mind," he confessed.

"Uh-huh," John said, nodding. "I thought so."

"Look, Dad—"

"Your mother and I married for the wrong reasons—okay, I married for the wrong reasons," John corrected himself. "That's the exception, son, not the rule."

"I wouldn't know. That's what I grew up with—no basis for comparison," he said coldly.

"I wish you hadn't..." John said tiredly. Then, "I wish you'd had the kind of terrific childhood every kid deserves. I wish I could have spared you the pain. There's a lot of things I'd do differently if I could, but I can't.''

Brian said nothing, suspecting there was more his father wanted to say.

''All I can do is tell you I'm sorry and urge you not to judge all marriages by mine,'' John said. ''For couples who do get married for the right reasons, marriage can be a wonderful thing.''

''You sound like Katie,'' Brian said with a twinge of amusement.

''Your sister's a good example,'' John said, nodding. ''She and Jerry have a great marriage.'' He paused. ''So did you and Elaine.''

''She and Jerry are something out of a sitcom.'' Brian chuckled. He didn't want to talk about Elaine.

''They're happy. That's the important thing,'' John insisted.

''Nobody could argue with that.''

''She didn't let my troubles scare her off,'' John said.

''Katie always was more of a risk-taker than I was,'' Brian reminded him.

''Some things are worth taking a chance on, son.''

''You know me, Dad. Always opt for the sure thing.''

John smiled patiently. ''There's no such thing as a sure thing,'' he said plainly. ''Everything in life is a gamble.''

"Some things more than others," Brian said, nodding in agreement.

"Ironically, the biggest risks are the ones worth taking," John said.

"So I've heard."

John's expression was serious. "Take it from someone who knows."

Why was she losing sleep over Brian Reynolds?

Amy still hadn't figured it out.

She'd tried. She'd been trying ever since she left Burke's Harbor. It didn't make any sense that he could rattle her like this.

It's not as if they were lovers or anything like that.

Lovers, Amy thought ruefully.

That's a laugh.

So why, she wondered, wasn't she laughing?

Much as she hated to admit it, she did have feelings for Brian Reynolds. Confused feelings at this point, but feelings nonetheless.

She'd come to realize that beneath that cloak of overpowering bitterness, he was a man who struggled with powerful emotions.

He could feel deep, genuine love...if only he'd let himself.

We don't even really like each other!

How many times had Brian told himself that since that incident down at the dock?

Incident!

He'd kissed her, for crying out loud!

He kissed me.

Had he done it to make her angry?

That didn't make sense. Nobody kissed out of anger. Did they?

Perhaps not, but he wasn't like anybody else.

Certainly not like anyone she had ever known.

Never in his life, he told himself.

Never had he ever met anybody like Amy.

She was an odd one, all right. Coming here as she did, approaching people she'd never met, looking for a man her mother hadn't seen in fifty years.

Some would call her a romantic.

I'd just call her a nut.

He's nuts, Amy decided.

A real loony.

He shuns marriage as if it's a serious criminal act.

But then, so did she.

He regards love as though it's an incurable illness.

But so did she.

The discovery unnerved her. It couldn't be.

It wasn't possible.

It's not possible.

He couldn't be.

Never in a million years could he fall for a woman like Amy. No, that just couldn't happen.

He couldn't fall in love at all, but definitely not with her.

She wasn't like any of the women he'd known, the women he'd dated.

Boy, was that the understatement of the year.

They had absolutely nothing in common, Amy reminded herself.

He's conservative. She was...well, she wasn't.

He grew up in a small town. She grew up in Boston.

He came from a broken home. Hers was stable.

He—

Amy stopped short.

She'd just realized that was really all she knew about him.

Except...

"She left?" Brian asked.

"You seem surprised," Katie noted as she tidied the bedroom Amy had planned to occupy while staying in Burke's Harbor.

"Well...yes, I am."

"She only came here for one thing," Katie reminded him. "She accomplished that. There was no reason for her to stay on. Was there?"

He looked at her. "What's that supposed to mean?"

"You tell me."

"You know I don't enjoy riddles, Katie." The tone of his voice made it clear that he was aggravated.

"What went on between you two?" she insisted.

"Amy Barrington and me?" he asked. "Absolutely nothing."

"That's not the way it looked to me." She looked—and sounded—totally unconvinced.

"And just *how* did it look to you, little sister?" he questioned her.

"Like you were starting to feel something for her that you didn't want to feel, and doing your level best to push her away." Katie summed up the relationship.

Brian laughed. "You have a very vivid imagination," he told her.

"And you protest too much."

"There was never anything of an even remotely romantic nature going on between us," he maintained.

"Then how do you explain what happened down at the dock?"

Brian couldn't hide his surprise. "You know about that?"

She nodded. "Amy told me."

His jaw tightened visibly. "What else did she tell you?" he asked, not really sure he wanted to know.

"Nothing, really. Just that you kissed her, but she

didn't expect it and didn't have a clue as to why you did it,'' Katie said with a shrug.

"That's all she said?"

"That's it," Katie stated. "Disappointed?"

"Of course not! Why should I be?" he asked irritably.

"I don't know. You just seem to be, that's all."

"I'm not."

"Fine. I'll take your word for it." Katie put fresh pillowcases on the pillows, white linen embroidered with a blue K.

"You don't believe me, do you?"

"I didn't say that."

"But you were thinking it."

"Now you're a clairvoyant?"

"Admit it, Katie," he challenged. "You think I have some kind of romantic feelings for Amy that I'm not confessing to."

Katie turned to face him, hands on her hips. "Did you hear me say those words to you?" she asked.

"No—"

"Then don't put words in my mouth to give yourself an excuse to bite my head off because you're frustrated."

"Frustrated?"

"Frustrated because you can't acknowledge your own feelings," Katie observed.

"See, I was right!" he retorted. "That *is* what you were thinking!"

''The important thing is what *you're* thinking and feeling,'' Katie stated. ''How do you really feel about her, Bri?''

He wouldn't answer at first, unwilling to open that particular Pandora's box, especially in the presence of his sister.

''Brian?''

''I don't know how I feel about her,'' he finally admitted.

''You don't know?''

''That's what I said, isn't it?''

''How can you not know how you feel, Brian?'' she asked.

''That's why I keep asking myself,'' he said sullenly.

''Want to talk about it?''

He shook his head. ''Not really.''

''It might help.'' She wouldn't give up. ''I might be able to see what you can't.''

''Right.''

''You don't trust me?''

''With my life,'' he assured her. ''But you have a history of meddling in my romantic involvements.''

''Romantic involvements? Is that what you call them?''

''What would you call them?'' he asked.

''I wouldn't call them romantic involvements,'' she said. ''Anything but. You've gone to incredible lengths to make sure they weren't.''

He shrugged. "None of those women was right for me."

"Did you even give them a chance?" Katie asked dubiously.

He didn't respond.

"I didn't think so." Katie paused. "What about Amy?"

"What about her?"

"Do you ever intend to find out how you feel about her?"

"I wonder if I wouldn't be better off not knowing," he said quietly.

Katie hesitated. "If you go through the rest of your life expecting the worst from everyone, that's exactly what you're going to get," she warned.

"What are you, a philosopher?" he asked.

But inside, he'd begun to wonder—about a lot of things.

"When do you think Dr. Jenkins will let me get back to living a normal life?" Marian asked her daughter.

"That's hard to say, Mom," Amy told her. "Brain surgery's not an exact science, you know."

Marian sighed heavily.

"Do you have something in particular in mind?" Amy asked.

Her mother nodded. "I'd like to go see John," she said.

Amy frowned. ''I think it's going to be a while before you'll be up to a long drive like that.''

''Perhaps by train—''

''Mom, Mom.'' Amy shook her head. ''Dr. Jenkins hasn't even given you the okay to leave the house yet, let alone leave the state.''

Marian's disappointment was written all over her face.

Amy's heart went out to her mother. ''Maybe he could come back here for another visit,'' she suggested.

''Do you think he could?'' Marian asked hopefully.

''There's one way to find out. I'll call him.''

''That would be wonderful—if he could,'' Marian said.

''Independence Day is coming up,'' Amy said. ''We could invite him for that. Maybe we could barbecue or something.''

Marian nodded. ''That would be nice. We haven't barbecued in a long time,'' she said.

We barbecued just before you went into the hospital, Mom, she thought. *You can't remember the immediate past, but you can vividly recall things that happened half a century ago?*

That's love.

''I'll call him today,'' she promised.

Marian nodded again.

Amy stayed with her mother until the older woman drifted off to sleep, then returned to her small office to at least try to work. That turned out to be impossible. She couldn't stop thinking about the promise she'd made to her mother.

Invite John for a barbecue.

If John comes, Brian will come with him, she thought.

Did she want to see Brian again?

Could she really be that starry-eyed?

She still hadn't sorted out her feelings where Brian Reynolds was concerned. It was like being in love with Dr. Jekyll and Mr. Hyde.

Love, she thought. How could she use the word love in the same sentence with Brian Reynolds?

It was like a bad joke.

Not that she didn't feel a strong attraction to him. She did. Even when he infuriated her most, it was there. But then, her judgment in that department hadn't exactly been the best, she thought. Parker proved that, didn't he?

She certainly didn't want to go through that again.

Yet a promise was a promise, she told herself.

She had to call John.

If Brian came with him, she'd deal with that if and when the time came. This is for Mom, she reminded herself. She deserves whatever happiness she can find with John.

She looked at the telephone. She might as well get it over with.

She considered calling Katie, leaving a message

with her. Chicken, she scolded herself. That would be so obvious.

Brian would know she was avoiding him.

Deciding to get this over with before she lost her nerve, she picked up the phone and dialed. To her relief, John answered.

"Hello?"

"John?"

"Yeah, this is John."

"This is Amy."

"Amy!" His voice warmed instantly. "Katie told me you'd gone home."

"I did," she said. "I'm calling from Boston."

"How's Marian?" he asked.

"Doing very well," she assured him. "That's why I'm calling, actually. Mom really wants to see you again."

"I want to see her, too."

"I was hoping you'd say that," she responded. "Independence Day is coming up..."

9

"I'm glad you could make it," Amy told Brian. *Do I mean that?*

He didn't smile. "I didn't have much of a choice." *To put it mildly.*

"I'm sorry you feel that way." *This was a big mistake. Big. Huge.*

"Katie usually has a big affair at the B and B," he informed her. It was the closest thing they'd ever had to a real family get-together. *And I had to miss it.*

"I didn't know." *But I'll bet you couldn't wait to tell me.*

He shrugged. "It's no big deal." *Too late to worry about it now.*

"Your father certainly seems happy to be here." *Too bad you're not more like your father.*

"There's nowhere else he'd rather be." *There never has been.*

"They love each other, Brian."

"I know that."

"Will you stand in their way if they decide they want to be together?" She had to know.

"I doubt if I could, even if I wanted to," he replied gravely.

"The question is, do you want to?"

He turned to look at her. "I don't know what I want," he answered honestly.

"Don't you want to find out?"

His smile was forced. "Sometimes I think I'm probably better off not knowing."

"How so?"

"There are times when I wonder what it would have been like to have had a normal life," he began. "A wife, kids—the kind of life my sister has."

"But?"

"Then I remind myself of the other possibility."

"The kind of marriage your parents had," she guessed.

He nodded.

There was a long silence before she spoke again. "I was married once," she said finally.

"'What happened?"

Amy frowned. "It took me a while to figure it out."

He gave her a quizzical look.

"I thought we had a good marriage. I was happy, and I thought he was, too—until he told me he wanted a divorce."

"You really didn't have a clue?"

"Nope."

"Why did he want a divorce?"

Her smile was sad. "As it turns out," she confided, "he was insecure. He couldn't deal with the success I was having as Adam McCabe."

"You earned more than he did," Brian concluded.

"Bingo."

"That's a real mature attitude."

She nodded. "He had an attitude, all right," she said.

"Must have been painful for you."

She nodded again. "When we split, I swore I'd never get married again," she told him.

"Looks like we're in the same boat."

"So it would seem," she said. "But lately I've begun to ask myself if I could have been wrong."

"About marriage?"

"All men can't possibly be like my ex-husband," she said with certainty. "Maybe I'm just being stupid. Maybe I've been stupid."

"I've had those feelings myself from time to time," he confessed.

"You?"

"You seem surprised."

"Well, frankly—I am," she said. "You've seemed so sure, so convinced that sort of thing wasn't in the cards for you."

"I've been trying to sell myself on it," he said. "Figured I'd be a lot better off unattached."

"We may both have been right."

"Maybe."

They both wondered if they'd live to regret the choices they'd made for themselves.

"We'll have to be going soon," Brian told Amy. He and John had already stayed in Boston two days longer than he'd intended.

"Do you have to?"

She seemed to really want him to stay, which came as a surprise to him. "Can't," he said regretfully. "I do have a business to run. Jerry's probably ready to shoot me now for not getting back when I said I would."

"I suppose."

He paused. "I *do* have another idea," he began.

"Oh?"

"Why don't you come back to Burke's Harbor?" he suggested. "At least for a while—"

She shook her head. "'I can't.'"

"Why not?"

"Mom. I can't leave her alone here," she reminded him. "And she's not up to a long drive. That's why I invited you and your dad here instead of taking her to Maine."

"Couldn't your sister stay with her again?" he asked.

Amy shook her head. "Patti's got a family of her

own out on Cape Cod. She can't just pick up and go for indefinite periods of time.''

"I see.''

She fell silent.

"There must be some way," he said finally.

Amy looked at him. "You really want me to come?" she asked.

"Isn't that what I've been saying?"

"Why?"

"Why have I been saying it?"

"No, why do you want me to come?" She wanted to know.

"That should be obvious."

"It's not."

He grimaced. "You're going to make me say it, aren't you?" he asked.

Amy nodded. "Yes."

"I've been thinking about what you said—about how you swore off marriage but wondered if that had been a mistake." He was talking fast, barely taking a breath between words. "Well, I've been wondering the same thing. I've been wondering if maybe you and I—that is, uh—maybe we should get to know each other better."

She was surprised. "You really want that?" she asked.

He nodded.

"I'll see what I can do."

* * *

"I don't believe it!"

"I'm not sure I believe it myself," Amy confessed that afternoon on the phone.

"You and Brian Reynolds," Patti said. Amy could visualize her shaking her head. "The two people on the planet least likely to get involved with anybody, let alone each other."

"Patti, we not involved."

"That's not how it sounds to me."

"Well, I can't help how it sounds or doesn't sound," Amy said firmly. "We're just sort of testing the waters at this point. We don't know if it's going to go anywhere or not."

"Oh, I see," Patti responded. "You want to find out if the two of you can stand to be in the same room with each other for more than five minutes before you decide if you want to tackle something more complicated, like a romance."

"Very funny."

"I thought so."

"So, will you do it?" Amy asked impatiently. "Will you come and stay with Mom so I can go?"

"That depends," Patti replied. "How long will you be gone?"

"Two weeks, maybe?"

Patti laughed. "Think you'll be able to tell in two weeks whether or not you're going to want a lifetime with the guy or not?" she asked dubiously.

"I'll have a clue, which is a lot more than I have now."

"All right," Patti said. "Two weeks—but that's the best I can do. I have a family waiting for me at home, remember?"

"Thanks, Pats. I owe you."

"You sure do—and you'd better believe I'll collect."

The restaurant overlooked the harbor. It was small, cozy, very romantic. It was also the site of a minor miracle in the making.

It was the first time Amy Barrington and Brian Reynolds spent more than an hour together without conflict.

"When Mom first told me about John, I had mixed feelings," Amy admitted. "On one hand, I wondered what it must be like to be loved like that—it was like something out of a fairy tale."

"And on the other hand?"

"On the other hand," she said with a heavy sigh, "it makes me wonder if she really loved my dad as much as I always thought she did."

"I sometimes wonder if there is such a thing," he said quietly, pushing the food around on his plate with his fork.

"As what?"

"Love."

Amy was thoughtful for a long moment. "I think

it's out there,'' she said finally. ''I just don't think it's all that easy to find.''

''For some of us, it's next to impossible,'' he told her.

''Maybe we're not looking in the right places,'' she suggested. ''Maybe we're just not working hard enough at it. I don't know.''

''I haven't been working at it at all,'' he confessed.

''So I hear.''

He raised an eyebrow. ''From who?'' he asked. ''Or do I even have to ask?''

She grinned. ''Your sister just wants you to be happy.''

''And to Katie, happiness is absolutely, positively impossible without a spouse and at least half a dozen kids.'' He chuckled.

''What's your idea of happiness?''

He shrugged. ''I don't know.''

''You must have some idea—''

''Nope.''

She gave him a disbelieving look. ''That's hard to believe.''

''Not really,'' he responded. ''I don't know what happiness is because I've never been happy.''

The next two weeks seemed to fly by, passing much more quickly than either Amy or Brian would have liked. They spent every free minute they had together—walking along the harbor, having dinner at the NoFrills seafood restaurant, sailing on his boat and talking.

Mostly talking.

Brian opened up to Amy as he had never opened up to anyone before. He talked about his hopes and dreams, his goals and interests—and he talked about his parents' stormy marriage and the profound effect it had on him, not only as a child, but later, as an adult. He talked about his late wife. Something he had never even discussed with his mother or Katie.

"I'm going to hate to have to leave here," Amy confided. "It's so beautiful, so peaceful here."

"Then don't leave. Stay."

"I can't. You know that."

"You need to get back to your mother," he said.

"She needs me."

"What about you, Amy?" he asked. "What about your needs?"

"I'll cross that bridge when I've figured out what my needs are," she told him.

"I think we'd both have a better chance of determining our needs if we did it together," he said.

"I'd love to stay, but I can't."

"Won't your sister stay with your mother—just a few more days?" he asked.

"She can't. She has a life of her own in Hyannisport."

"And because she has a life, you're not entitled to one?"

''No, it's not like that at all,'' she insisted. ''It's just not easy for her to pick up and go with a husband and children.''

''So responsibility for your mother falls solely to you,'' he concluded, a hint of resentment in his voice.

''I moved in with Mom because I wanted to,'' she assured him. ''I love her. I wanted to be there for her—the way she was there for me when I was growing up.''

''The way my mother was there for me when I was growing up,'' Brian said quietly.

''You do understand, then.'' Half statement, half question.

He nodded. ''I understand,'' he assured her. ''I just don't want you to leave, that's all.''

''So, how's it going?'' Patti asked, propping the receiver on her shoulder as she sat up to switch on the bedside light.

''Hard to tell,'' Amy said, flopping down on the bed and kicking off her shoes.

''What's that supposed to mean?''

''Just what I said. At the moment, it's hard to tell,'' Amy repeated, her fingers absently tracing the blue-embroidered K on the white linen pillowcase. ''I've seen a side of him I wouldn't have believed existed a month ago.''

''Then he is human?''

''Patti, really.''

"Well, I wasn't quite sure."

"He's been wonderful, Pats."

"But?"

"But he still has doubts," Amy said, swatting the pillow. "And he still has a problem with the idea of Mom and John being together."

"You think that could be a problem between the two of you?"

"I don't see how it could not be a problem," Amy said worriedly. "How can he separate the daughter from the mother?"

"I wouldn't expect him to change overnight," Patti cautioned. "He's lived with this most of his life, after all."

"That's what I'm afraid of."

There was a brief silence on the other end of the line. "You're falling in love with him, aren't you?" Patti finally asked.

"I'm not sure," Amy answered truthfully, sitting up straighter now. "I think I am—I think I could be."

I'm in love with her.

Brian wasn't sure he was entirely. What had he gotten himself into?

He rubbed his temples, willing his headache to go away—but knowing it wouldn't. It would be with him until he made up his mind about Amy.

Falling in love with Marian Haskell's daughter was

the last thing he'd expected to do, the last thing he'd wanted to do.

Talk about sleeping with the enemy, he thought miserably.

Though he told himself Amy wasn't the enemy. How could she be? She was Marian Haskell's daughter, but she hadn't even been born when her mother and his father fell in love.

Still, he thought, feeling the way he did about her mother, how could he ever expect to have any kind of a future with Amy?

Eventually, it was bound to come between them.

Do I want to risk that?

The answer was an unqualified no. He'd spent most of his adult life avoiding commitment because he couldn't handle the possibility of history repeating itself. He was no more prepared for that now than he'd ever been.

Until he could put aside his feelings about Marian and John, there was no chance for a future with Amy.

10

"It's out of the question, Dad!"

"When did you become my keeper, Brian?" John demanded angrily.

"This is too much," Brian stated. "You know what Doc Eberhardt said—"

"Bull!" John snorted. "This isn't about my health and you know it!"

Brian ignored that last statement. "You have to face reality, Dad—you're not a young man anymore."

"No, I'm not. I'm an old man!" John rasped. "I'm old enough to make my own decisions, not have my son make them for me!"

"I'm only thinking of you," Brian insisted.

"Don't give me that!" John snapped. "You're only thinking of yourself. You don't want Marian and me to be together, so you come up with any excuse you can to prevent it. But it isn't going to work, do you hear me?"

"Dad—"

"Don't 'Dad' me, Brian Reynolds!" John shouted. "If I want to go to Boston, I'll go—with or without you!" He got up and headed for the door.

"Dad—wait!" Brian called after him.

John didn't respond. He just kept walking.

Will Brian ever get over it?

Amy had her doubts.

He'd lived with the bitterness, the anger, for so long—no, he hadn't just lived with it, he'd fed it, nurtured it—that she had to wonder if he'd ever really be free of it.

She wasn't fighting a losing battle, Amy told herself.

It was an admission she hated to make, because for the first time since her divorce, she found herself actually caring. She'd met a man she could fall in love with.

A love that has no future, she thought sadly. None.

Of all the men she could have fallen for, why did she have to pick the son of the man her mother had once loved, probably still loved—a man who blamed her mother for all of his unhappiness?

No point in sticking around, she thought miserably.

"What's the problem?" Amy asked.

Brian frowned. "Is it that obvious?" he asked.

"Only a billboard could be more obvious," she told him.

"Great."

"Want to talk about it?"

He shook his head. "Not really."

Amy paused. "Let me guess. It has to do with your father and my mother," she concluded, hoping she was wrong.

Brian nodded. "He wants to make another trip to Boston."

"And you don't want him to."

"No," he reluctantly confessed.

"You still have problems with their relationship," Amy ventured.

"Yeah." He drew in his breath. "I've tried not to, but I do."

Amy was quiet for a moment. "Do you think that's ever going to change?" she asked.

"I'm trying, Amy," was the only reassurance he could offer her.

"I have to wonder if that's going to be enough," she worried out loud.

"Rationally, I know I'm being unreasonable," he admitted. "But another part of me—"

"Another part of you is still that ten-year-old boy who cried himself to sleep listening to his parents fight," she finished the sentence for him.

He nodded. "Until the divorce, anyway. I'm really

sorry, Amy. But I can't help thinking that their marriage could have worked, that he could have loved her, if he hadn't met your mother,'' he said quietly.

"Brian, do you intend to spend the rest of your life living in the past?" She wanted to know. Needed to know.

"Amy, please—"

"Brian, I love my mother. I want her to be happy," she told him honestly. "If John can make her happy, if they can make each other happy, then I want them to be together."

"What about your father?"

"What about him?"

"Didn't he matter at all to you?"

"I loved my father!" Amy was appalled that he would even suggest such a thing."

"Surely he was hurt, too, by this great love affair—"

"No, he was not!" Amy snapped. "My mother loved my father! They had a good marriage. Mom never even mentioned John to Patti and me until after Dad died!"

"Then you were better off than I was!" He turned and walked away.

"Brian, wait!" she called after him. This was getting them nowhere.

He waved her off. "There's someone I have to

see—now!'' he called over his shoulder. ''I'll call you when I get back.''

''How's Mom?''

''The doctor says she's making remarkable progress,'' Patti reported. ''He can't believe it.''

''That's great.''

There was a pause on the other end of the line. ''Amy, are you all right?'' her sister asked.

''Sure. Why do you ask?''

''I don't know. You just sound funny,'' Patti told her.

''I'm tired, that's all.''

''Are you sure?''

''I may be home soon,'' Amy said then.

''Oh?''

''The two weeks are almost up,'' Amy reminded her.

''I know,'' Patti began slowly, ''but somehow I expected you to call saying you need more time.''

''That would be pointless.''

''Things aren't going well between you and Prince Charming?''

''Things aren't going well, period.''

''I'm sorry.''

''Me, too.'' Amy paused. ''It was a mistake. I should have known better.''

Next time I will.

"Brian! Why didn't you tell me you were coming?" his mother asked.

He grinned. "I wanted to surprise you."

"Well, you certainly did that!" She stood to give her son a proper greeting, a kiss and a hug. "You will stay for dinner, won't you?"

"Why do you think I'm here?" he joked. "I miss your home-cooked meals—you know that."

"Oh, come now. I happen to know that Katherine is an excellent cook."

"Not as good as you," Brian told her. "Besides, she's got her hands full with the B and B. The last thing she needs is two more mouths to feed."

Rhonda Reynolds smiled. "You and John haven't yet developed the basic survival skills in the kitchen, I take it," she concluded, amused.

"I can open a can and Dad can boil water," Brian confessed.

"Men!" She laughed.

Brian paused. "Mom, we need to talk," he said finally.

"Suddenly so serious," his mother observed. "You didn't just come for a visit, did you?"

He shook his head.

"There's a problem?"

"In a way." He led her back to the couch. He had to tell her before he lost his nerve. "There's something I need to tell you before you hear it from someone else.''

Her smile vanished. ''It sounds serious,'' she said, sitting down.

''It's about Marian Barrington—Marian Haskell, I mean.''

She looked puzzled. ''That was a long time ago, Brian,'' she said.

He shook his head. ''She's back in his life.'' He went on to tell her about the letter that was lost in the mail, Amy showing up in Burke's Harbor and the reunion in Boston.

''He always did love her,'' Rhonda said when he had finished.

''I know.''

She paused. ''What about you?''

''What about me?''

''How do you feel about it?''

''How do you think I feel?''

She shook her head. ''What have I done to you?'' she wondered out loud.

He looked confused. ''You?''

''When your father and I were still together, I was so desperately unhappy that I didn't stop to think about what I was doing to you,'' she said sadly.

''Mom, you're not making sense,'' he said, confused.

''Of course I am.'' Her eyes met his. ''I made you

so unhappy as a child—that's why you've never re-married, isn't it?''

He shook his head. "If Dad had been the kind of husband he should have been..." he began.

"No, Brian. It was my fault."

"No."

"Yes," she said firmly. "I should never have married him. I knew he was on the rebound."

"You loved him."

"Yes, I did,'' she said, "but he didn't love me, and I knew he didn't love me. I took advantage of the pain he was feeling over losing her to get him to marry me."

"Mom—"

"I thought I could change that," she went on. "I thought that once we were married, I could make him love me. I thought I could make him happy. I should have known better."

"Why are you telling me this now?" he asked.

"Because I want you to be happy," she answered honestly. "You're all alone now. I know that's my fault."

"No, Mom—"

"Yes, it is," she interrupted. "I know only too well that our battles left you with most of the scars."

"That wasn't your fault."

"Yes, it was. Your father wanted to keep you out of our arguments," she said. "I drew you into them because I could count on you to take my side. I took comfort in that.''

''You were hurting.''

''That was no excuse.'' She paused. ''I've loved your father since we were kids. There was never anyone else for me. But if I'd had half a brain, I wouldn't have married him, knowing he didn't feel the same way.''

He frowned, saying nothing.

''Him finding her again—he's finally got what he's always wanted,'' Rhonda said then. ''I would imagine he's very happy.''

''Walking on air.'' There was a twinge of sarcasm in Brian's voice.

''Are they planning to be married?''

''Dad hasn't said anything, but I'm sure he's thinking about it.''

''I'm sure he is.'' She was silent for a long moment. ''Don't let it make you bitter, Brian.''

''How can I not?''

''Because, my darling, our troubles were ours, not yours,'' she told him. ''Just because I made a bad marriage doesn't mean you will.''

''It doesn't mean I won't, either.''

''You know, in spite of everything, I can't say I'm sorry I married your father,'' she said. ''Something truly wonderful did come out of that union.''

''I can't imagine what.''

"You and your sister," his mother said. "That's what."

Brian was still thinking about their conversation when he got home later that night. It was ironic that the one thing his parents seemed to be in agreement about was that their marriage had been a monumental failure.

Actually, he thought, *they agree on a few other things, too.*

Like me.

They think I'm being an idiot.

They may be right.

"Dad?" he called. He needed to see his father, needed to talk to him.

No response.

"Dad!"

He looked at his watch. It was past midnight. Surely his father hadn't gone out, not this late. He was usually sound asleep by ten.

"Dad!"

Still no answer.

Thinking he might have gone to bed instead of falling asleep in front of the TV as he normally did, Brian went upstairs to check.

John was not in his room.

Now Brian was worried.

He couldn't have gone far. *Think,* Brian prodded

himself. Where could he have gone this time of the night?

They'd argued earlier. Argued about Marian, about Amy. Normally, he went out to cool off when they had an argument.

The Veterans of Foreign Wars hall, he thought. His usual cooling-off place.

Nothing improved his father's bad moods more than an evening with his cronies, reminiscing over a few beers. Usually a few more than John's doctor would have liked him to have.

He picked up the phone on the nightstand and dialed the number for the VFW hall. It took only a minute to find out that John wasn't there.

Back to square one.

He called the bed and breakfast. Katie answered the phone. "Kirks' Bed and Breakfast."

"Katie, it's Brian."

"Brian? What's up?"

"Is Dad there with you?"

"Dad? At this hour?" she asked. "You know better than that."

"What I don't know is where our father is right now," he told her. "I was hoping he was with you."

"I haven't seen him since this morning," she said. "Have you tried the VFW hall?"

"Yeah."

"He's not there?"

"No, he's not."

Brian turned to open the closet door. His father's beat-up old suitcase was gone. "He's left," Brian said.

"Left what?"

"The house. Burke's Harbor," Brian said. "His suitcase is gone."

"Where would he go?"

"It doesn't take a rocket scientist to figure that one out."

"You think he went to Boston?"

"I'd bet money on it."

"I don't see how he could have," Katie told him. "He couldn't have gone on his own. Amy's still here."

"She is? Is she in her room?"

"Yes, but—"

"Connect me with her room."

"I think she's probably asleep."

"Just put me through."

11

───►◄───

"Is he with you?" Brian demanded angrily.

"What?" Amy asked, confused, struggling to rouse herself from a sound sleep.

"My father. Is he with you?"

"No!" she responded irritably. "Why would he be with me?"

"Hitching a ride to Boston, maybe?" he suggested acidly.

"Oh, please!"

"Are you denying it's possible?"

"I'm not denying anything!" She sat up in bed. "I don't have to defend myself to you—or anyone else, for that matter!"

"You're telling me you haven't seen him, then?"

"I'm not telling you anything." She hung up.

Less than a minute later, the phone rang. She snatched it up. "I told you—"

"Amy?"

It was her sister's voice on the other end of the

line. "Patti?" she asked, suddenly anxious. Her sister, calling at this hour? "Mom—is she—"

"Mom's fine," Patti assured her. "It's just that—"

"What?"

"We just got a call. From Mr. Reynolds," Patti told her.

"Brian called you?"

"Not Brian. His father."

Amy ran one hand through her hair. "John. Where is he?"

There was a brief pause on the other end. "I don't know where he is," Patti said. "But I do know where he's going to be."

"He's coming there?"

"That's what he says."

"When?"

"He didn't say exactly when he'd be here," Patti replied. "I don't think he was sure. He just said he wanted to see Mom."

"And?"

"I told him she was anxious to see him, too," Patti went on. "He said he'd be here as soon as he could."

"Did he talk to Mom?"

"No. She was asleep," Patti said. "I told her when she woke up."

"I'll be there as soon as I can," Amy informed her.

"Is there a problem?"

"There might be," Amy said, "if Brian gets there before I do."

At that point their conversation was interrupted by someone pounding on her door. She didn't have to be clairvoyant to know who it was. "Got to go," she told her sister.

She hung up and went to open the door. "Do you always barge in on your sister's guests in the middle of the night like this?" she asked.

Brian looked as though he might very well explode. "None of her other guests has caused as much trouble as you have," he growled as he entered the room.

"He's not here," she told him again.

He didn't respond.

"Want to look under the bed?"

"You know where he is."

Her eyes met his defiantly. "If I did, I wouldn't tell you," she assured him.

"He's in Boston, isn't he?"

"No," Amy answered truthfully.

"But that's where he's headed," Brian concluded as his eyes scanned the room, looking everywhere but at her.

"If you'll calm down and at least try to pretend to be a rational human being, I'll try to help you find him," Amy offered.

"What makes you think I need—or want—your help?" he responded irritably, still avoiding her eyes.

"You're here, aren't you?"

He ignored her question. "It's obvious where he's going and why," he said tightly.

"He wouldn't have to keep running away like a disobedient child if you'd treat him like the grown man he is and respect his right to do as he pleases," Amy stated flatly.

"He's not a well man!" Brian snapped. "And certainly too old for this Romeo and Juliet crap!"

"How do you know that?" Amy challenged. "Are you so miserable that you can't stand the thought of your father finding happiness?"

"Now just a minute—"

"You've resigned yourself to a life alone, so you want to saddle your father with the same sorry existence—is that it?"

He glared at her. "You're a fine one to talk!" he mocked. "You're doing exactly the same thing."

"Oh, please—" she began.

"What would you call it?" he demanded. "Your marriage failed, so you never took a chance on another man."

"That's hardly the same thing."

"That's exactly the same thing," he argued. "We're both skeptics, you and I. Neither of us really believes in happily-ever-after."

"I do believe in happily-ever-after!" she retorted. "I can't help it if the man I love doesn't!"

"The man you— What?" He stared at her, not sure he believed what he'd just heard.

"You, you big jerk—I'm talking about you!" She couldn't believe she'd actually blurted it out, she thought, horrified. She couldn't believe she was admitting it after all that had happened—all that was wrong between them.

He was staggered. "Are y-you saying—" he stammered, unable to finish.

Amy's face flushed. "I think I already said it," she replied uneasily.

"Did you mean it?"

She avoided his eyes. "I wish I didn't," she said quietly.

He stiffened. "Why?"

"That should be obvious," she said. "I feel like such a fool."

"Don't." He reached out, placing his hands on her shoulders.

She shook him off. "My judgment really stinks," she complained. "First a bad marriage, and now this."

"'This' meaning a man who's a colossal waste of your time and energies because he's too damned stubborn to see what he's missing," he said. "Am I close?"

She nodded, still refusing to look at him. "That pretty much covers it, yes," she replied in a barely audible voice.

"I love you, Amy."

"Look, I know this is really stupid—" She stopped

short, looking up at him for the first time. "Wait a minute! Did you say—"

He nodded, laughing. "I said I love you. And..." he added, "I really meant it." Impulsively, he kissed her.

She stared at him in disbelief. "This isn't funny, Brian."

"I agree." He was still laughing. "I think we ought to do something about it." He kissed her again, but she still wasn't taking him seriously.

"Like what?" she asked, not entirely sure she wanted to hear his answer.

He drew in a deep breath. "Like get married, maybe."

"What's the catch?"

"No catch. Well, maybe just one," he confessed.

"Right." She eyed him suspiciously. "And that condition is?"

"We'd have to live here in Burke's Harbor," he told her. "After all, I have a business to run here."

She nodded. "We'd be living at your house?" she asked, still stunned by his unexpected admission.

He grinned sheepishly. "Well, actually, that's my father's home," he confessed. "But I'm sure we can find something—"

"Near the water?"

"If that's what you want."

"With a room where I can work?"

"Of course."

"With a window facing the harbor?"

He laughed out loud. "You are picky, aren't you?" he quipped.

"Well?"

He surrendered. "If it doesn't have one, I'll put one in."

"What about my mother?"

He smiled. "I don't think you'll have to worry about your mother being alone," he said. Then he kissed her again—and this time, she knew he meant it.

The bus station at South Berwick, Maine, was almost deserted when Amy and Brian arrived. A quick scan of the station turned up nothing, so while Brian went outside to talk to the drivers waiting to depart, Amy took a photograph of John to the ticket agent.

"Have you seen this gentleman?"

The man took the photograph from her and studied it for a long moment. "Yeah," he said finally, nodding. "I've seen him."

"When?" Amy asked anxiously.

"Earlier this evening. I sold him a ticket," he remembered.

"To Boston?"

He nodded again. "As a matter of fact, yes," he replied.

"When did the bus leave?"

He looked at his watch. "A little over an hour ago—12:15."

"Where does it stop next?"

He checked the schedule. "That would be Manchester," he said. "New Hampshire."

"New Hampshire!"

The ticket agent shrugged. "He missed the last direct to Boston, said he didn't want to wait until morning for the next one," he said. "I put him on a connecting line."

"To where?"

He checked again. "Buffalo."

"Where would he change buses, then?" she asked.

"Manchester," he said. "He'd have a forty-five minute layover there. He'll catch the bus to Boston originating in Montpelier, Vermont."

"Thank you," she said, taking the copy of the schedule he offered her. "Thank you very much."

She ran outside to find Brian. He was talking to one of the drivers when she found him.

"He's not here," she told him. "He got on a bus headed for Manchester—New Hampshire. The ticket agent said he's supposed to connect there with a bus going to Boston."

Brian nodded. "Let's go."

They ran all the way back to the lot where Brian's Jeep was parked. Brian pushed the speed limit all the way to Manchester.

"If we get pulled over, we'll never get there in time," Amy worried out loud.

"At least we know where he's going," Brian said. "We always knew that."

"True. But now we know how he's getting there."

"Maybe we should just let him go, catch up with him in Boston," Amy suggested.

Brian shook his head. "Not a good idea," he disagreed.

"Why not? It's obviously what he wants."

"There are things about Dad you don't know, Amy," he said.

"Like what?"

"Like he's not well," Brian said. "He's been in the hospital a couple of times—for his heart."

"How bad is it?" Amy asked, suddenly concerned.

"Pretty bad." He was silent for a moment. "He can't get it through his thick head that there are a lot of things he just can't do anymore."

"It's hard for just about anyone to accept that age or health problems make them incapable of doing all they might want to do." Amy was thinking of her mother, of how hard it had been for Marian to adjust to having to rely on others, however temporarily.

"Dad hasn't accepted it at all."

Another source of tension between them, Amy concluded silently.

"Because of the existing problems between us, he

took every attempt on my part to protect him as an attempt to imprison him,'' Brian told her.

"I can imagine.'' That was the truth. She could.

"The harder I try to make him take it easy, the more stubborn he gets,'' Brian confided. "The more determined he is to do as he pleases.''

"Maybe if they were together, they wouldn't be so cantankerous,'' Amy said then.

"What?'' He obviously hadn't been listening, focusing all of his attention on the road.

"Your father and my mother,'' Amy said. "If they were together, maybe they'd be better off.''

He nodded. "That's what I've been thinking.''

She smiled. "I don't believe it.''

He grinned. "Don't believe what?''

"That you may actually be willing to give those two a chance.''

He reached out and took her hand. "Maybe getting to know her daughter has given me a new outlook,'' he said. "Maybe I'm just beginning to see what I've been missing.''

She turned to look at him in the darkness. "What we've both been missing,'' she corrected.

At the bus station in Manchester, Amy went to the ticket counter first to make sure the bus hadn't departed. "Not yet,'' the agent told her. "It'll be boarding in about ten minutes.''

"Thanks.''

Dodging suitcase-laden travelers, she made her way through rows of uncomfortable-looking chairs equipped with small, coin-operated TV sets, looking for Brian, looking for John—but finding neither one.

Deciding Brian was probably outside where the buses were parked, she went out to look. Brian was there, heading toward her.

"Any luck?" she called.

He shook his head. "The bus is out here but hasn't started to board yet," he said. "I don't know where else he could be."

Amy stepped aside so he could pass through the glass doors, then followed him back inside. "Think he could be in the coffee shop?" she suggested.

"It's the only place we haven't looked," he said.

They found him there, sitting alone in a booth, finishing a cup of coffee. When he saw Brian, he was immediately on the defensive.

"I'm not going back," he insisted. "You wasted your time chasin' me down."

"I came after you because I'm worried about you, Dad," Brian tried to tell him.

"Yeah, right!" the older man snorted.

"It's the truth, John," Amy told him. "We didn't come to take you back to Burke's Harbor."

"Good thing," he growled. "I'm not going, no matter what."

She smiled patiently. "We came to take you on to Boston."

His eyes moved from her to Brian and back again. "This isn't some kind of trick, is it?"

Brian laughed. "No, Dad, it's not a trick. I swear it's not."

John nodded, getting to his feet. "I guess I can trust you—as long as she's with you," he conceded with a nod at Amy's smiling face.

"Thanks for the vote of confidence, Dad," Brian said, rolling his eyes skyward as he picked up John's suitcase and followed them out of the coffee shop.

They were halfway to Boston when it started to rain. John had fallen asleep in the back seat.

"He's really worn-out," Amy observed.

"All too easily these days," Brian said in a worried tone. "Unfortunately, I can't make him believe it."

"I've had the same problem with Mom since her surgery," Amy told him.

"So you figure if they were together, then—"

"They'd be more content," Amy finished.

"More willing to stay put."

"Exactly."

He thought about it for a few moments. "It's worth a shot," he said finally. "It certainly worked for me."

Amy raised an eyebrow. "Did it, now?" she asked in a mildly playful tone.

"I never thought I'd ever let myself fall in love…no holds barred," he confessed.

"What changed your mind?"

"You did."

She laughed. "There has to be more to it than that," she said.

"Yeah? What makes you think so?"

"For one thing, I've been up there in Burke's Harbor for weeks now—and you've spent most of that time trying to get me to leave," she reminded him.

"It wasn't all bad!" he responded defensively.

"No, it wasn't," she agreed. "But every time we started to get close and things would start to be good between us, you'd do a sudden about-face and be more determined than ever to run me out of town."

"Couldn't you tell I was scared?"

"Scared?"

"Yeah—scared!"

"No," she admitted, shaking her head. "I knew there was something going on with you, but I never thought you were scared. I just thought you had an evil twin or something."

"Very funny."

"I didn't know what to make of you," she confessed. "Your moods were about as unpredictable as the weather."

He kept his eyes on the road. "Like I said, I was scared."

"Scared."

"Yeah."

"Okay."

"You think I couldn't be?"

"You, afraid of me? No, I don't." She knew what he was getting at, but she wanted him to admit it.

She wanted him to say the words.

"I wasn't afraid of you, exactly," he said, obviously uncomfortable.

"No?"

He turned to look at her. "You're not going to make this easy for me, are you?" he asked, returning his eyes to the road in front of him.

She smiled. "No, I'm not."

He made a face. "I didn't think so."

It was raining so hard he could barely see to drive. "Think we should pull over somewhere and wait it out?" he asked.

"Stop changing the subject."

"I'm not. Look, see for yourself!"

"I can't see a thing."

"Exactly."

"All right, stop somewhere."

"Big of you," he mumbled.

"What?"

"Nothing."

"I'll bet."

He parked on the first parking lot they came to. It turned out to be the parking lot of a restaurant. "Want to go inside?" Brian asked.

She was wary. "Think we'll make it without life jackets?"

"If we make a run for it."

John woke up then. "What's going on?" he asked. "Why have we stopped?"

"We're waiting for the rain to let up," Brian told him, gesturing toward the windshield.

"Let's go in," John said promptly. "I'm hungry."

Brian grinned at Amy. "Looks like you're outnumbered, sweetheart," he said, feigning regret.

"You're not off the hook," she told him as they prepared to make a run for it.

He gave her an even broader grin. "Thanks for the warning."

12

"The rain seems to be letting up," Amy said, peering through the windows into the darkness.

Brian nodded. "Think maybe we should go while we can?" he asked, finishing his coffee.

"Might be a good idea."

"What might be a good idea," John growled, "would be to get our butts in gear and hit the road before we end up caught in another downpour." He proceeded to wrap a half-eaten jelly doughnut in a napkin and tuck it into the pocket of his beat-up old bomber jacket.

Amy and Brian looked at each other. "I think we've been given our orders," Brian said with a grin.

Amy nodded. "I guess so."

He helped her into her raincoat, then went up to the cash register to pay the bill. "I'll go get the Jeep and bring it up to the door," he told them.

"You'll get no argument from me," Amy assured him.

"Think we could go today?" John asked, clearly annoyed.

Brian's eyes rolled skyward. "Yes, Dad," he groaned.

"Sometimes I worry about that boy," John told Amy as they watched Brian dash through the rain to the Jeep.

Amy laughed. "He's hardly a boy, John," she told him.

"He'll always be a boy to me."

"I'm sure," Amy said, amused. "What makes you worry about him?"

"That ought to be obvious."

Amy said nothing, waiting for him to go on.

"He's been so cynical all his life," John said, not telling her anything she hadn't already suspected. "Even as a kid, he was miserable."

"He had a hard time with the divorce." Amy looked toward the parking lot. Brian seemed to be having trouble starting the Jeep.

"He resented me for not being able to make his mother happy, for not keeping the family together," John said, frowning.

"It's made it hard for him to trust, to let himself care," Amy said.

John looked at her. "He's talked to you about it?"

Amy nodded. "To an extent."

John couldn't hide his surprise. "He usually doesn't confide in anybody," he told her.

"I don't doubt that."

"The two of you must be getting pretty close," he guessed.

"You could say that." She paused. "He's asked me to marry him, John," she confided.

"Wha— Well, I'll be!" The older man's face broke into a huge grin. "I had no idea!"

"Neither did I," she admitted.

He looked confused now. "Huh?"

"Every time I felt like we were getting close, he'd just do an abrupt turnaround and retreat," she said.

John shook his head. "His mom and I didn't work, and after Elaine died, he was convinced no marriage could work," he said. "I never could get it through that thick head of his that we didn't work because we just didn't belong together."

Amy could see that Brian was under the hood now.

"He told me your ex-wife had always been in love with you," Amy said, watching Brian through the window, wondering what the problem could be.

John sucked in a breath. "Yeah, I guess she was," he said quietly.

"He said the two of you grew up together," she recalled.

"Pretty much, yeah. In fact, we never dated anybody else," he said, "until that summer I went to New York."

"And met my mother."

He nodded.

"So she really did come between you," Amy concluded.

"No, not exactly."

She raised an eyebrow.

"I never loved Rhonda the way she loved me," John said with a twinge of regret in his voice. "I cared about her, I just wasn't in love with her. I never intended to marry her."

"Why did you then?"

He frowned. "Rejection's a hard thing to take," he confessed. "When your mother didn't answer my letter, I felt about as low as it's possible to feel. When I came home, Rhonda was there. I knew how she felt, I knew she wouldn't reject me."

"So you married her."

"Yeah."

"Didn't you think about how it would hurt her?" Amy asked.

"Hurt her?" He shook his head. "No, I thought I was doing what she wanted."

"Even though you didn't love her?"

"I was a good husband," he stated defensively. "I was always home when I wasn't working. I never cheated on her."

"Except in your heart."

"Huh?"

"You were in love with someone else." Amy looked up. "Looks like Brian finally got the Jeep started. We'd better go out there."

John looked relieved.

"Why didn't you call to let me know you were coming?" Patti whispered to Amy as soon as they were reasonably alone.

"You made it abundantly clear that you didn't want to be called in the middle of the night," Amy proclaimed innocently.

Patti made a face. "Since when has that ever stopped you?"

"Come on, Pats, lighten up," Amy urged. "We're planning a wedding here. Probably two."

"A wedding—"

"Brian asked me to marry him."

"That's great—wait a minute!" Patti stopped short. "Let me guess. Like an idiot, you said no."

Amy gave her an indignant look. "I'm not that stupid."

"You said yes?"

"Of course I did."

"That's great—I think."

Amy laughed. "Make up your mind, Pats." She smiled at her sister.

"I'm happy for you. I am," Patti assured her.

"You just didn't believe it would ever happen," Amy concluded.

"Truthfully—no."

"Thanks for the vote of confidence."

"You forget—I know you."

Amy playfully punched her arm.

"And what's this about 'probably two'?" Patti asked, suddenly remembering the rest of Amy's announcement.

"I think John's going to pop the question to Mom," Amy told her.

Patti looked worried. "Do you think she's up to that?"

"I think this is the best thing that could happen to her," Amy said confidently.

"Hey, should I be worried?" Brian interrupted.

Amy gave him a peck on the cheek. "Worried? About what?"

"You two here in a huddle, talking about me behind my back," he said, returning Amy's kiss.

"What makes you think we're talking about you?" Amy asked.

"What else could you be talking about?" he replied, grinning.

"Such arrogance!" Amy laughed.

Patti looked past him. "Where's your dad, Brian?" she asked.

He turned. "I guess he couldn't wait," he concluded.

"Couldn't wait?" Patti asked.

Brian nodded. "He probably went up to pop the question."

"Mom's still asleep." Patti started to follow him, but Amy stopped her.

"They've waited fifty years for this, Pats," she said. "I don't think Mom will mind missing an hour's sleep."

She certainly hadn't.

"Marian, wake up!" John urged.

She began to stir. Blinking twice, she opened her eyes and looked up at him. "John." She spoke his name in a sleep-filled voice. "What are you doing here?"

"Something I tried to do over fifty years ago," he told her.

"What?"

She tried to sit up, but he stopped her. "Don't," he told her. "Just listen, okay?"

She nodded.

"I want to marry you, Marian."

"John—are you sure?" she questioned.

"After all these years? I've never been so sure." He paused. "Aren't you?"

"Yes," she told him. "But it's been such a long time…"

He smiled. "Too long," he said. "We have a lot of lost time to make up for."

"I do love you."

"And I love you. So what do you say, kiddo?" he asked. "Are we worth a second chance, or not?"

"Yes." Tears filled her eyes now. "I say yes!"

He bent to kiss her. "Better late than never, kiddo."

"This jacket—it must be forty, fifty years old..."

He grinned. "I wore it during the war," he said. "I was wearing it the first time I proposed to you. The day I mailed that letter," he explained, fingering the soft, worn leather with pride.

Marian smiled. "Some things never change," she said softly.

"Like us?"

"Like us," she said, nodding. "But mostly, like you, John."

He raised an eyebrow.

"Once the romantic, always the romantic," she told him. "Even now, after all these years."

"We should set a date," he said.

She nodded in agreement. "When do you think would be a good time?"

He gave her a wicked grin. "How about D day?" he suggested.

"Be serious!" she scolded him.

"I am," he insisted. "It does seem appropriate, if you think about it. Though it is almost a year away."

"I don't want a lot of fuss," she said then. "Family and a few friends, at the most."

"I agree," he said, "but—"

"But what?"

"Brian and Amy might have other ideas," he admitted.

"Brian and Amy? What do they have to do with this?" Marian asked.

"They're getting married, too."

"So when do you want to do the deed?" Brian asked.

Amy laughed. "'Do the deed'?"

"You know, get married."

They were walking, arms around each other, in the Boston Common. It was early afternoon, and they'd come for lunch after a few hours of much-needed sleep. A mounted patrolman rode past them, as did a group of children on bicycles. A magician performed to a small but enthusiastic audience near the Frog Pond, pulling a white rabbit from a very large top hat.

"You make it sound like a life sentence," she observed wryly.

"I do not!"

"You talk about setting a date with all the enthusiasm of a rodeo cowboy trying to walk in new boots a size too small," she told him.

"Reflex," he insisted stubbornly. "Old habits are hard to break."

"Maybe we should opt for a long engagement," she said after a moment's pause.

"Why would you want to do that?" he asked, concerned.

"I thought you might want to."

"Well, I don't."

"Are you sure?"

"Are you trying to end the marriage before we even say our 'I do's'?" he queried.

"Of course not!" she responded, surprised. "I just want you to be sure, that's all."

"That's all?"

She nodded. "I've been in divorce court once," she said. "I have absolutely no desire to do it again."

"I've never been in court, but I have been a victim of a divorce, and I'm not about to go through it again. When we get married, I intend it to be for good," he promised.

Amy was silent for a moment. *I've got my work cut out for me,* she thought. Even though he'd told her he loved her, even though he'd asked her to marry him, it didn't mean all the doubts and fears of a lifetime were going to just disappear like magic. How did he put it? "Old habits are hard to break"? *Some old habits are impossible to break—nobody knows that better than I do,* she told herself. *But we love each other enough to deal with anything.*

Out loud she said, "How about, say, Valentine's Day?"

"Nope," he said, shaking his head. "Too far off."

"New Year's Eve?"

"Still too far off."

"Christmas Eve?"

"Please!"

"Thanksgiving?"

He shook his head.

She was exasperated. "Don't tell me you want to get married next week!"

He grinned. "Actually, I was thinking of Saturday."

"Impossible!"

"Not if we elope."

"Elope!" It came out a shriek. "Listen, honey—if we don't get married in front of at least a few reliable witnesses, with our track records in the marriage department, nobody's going to believe we really 'did the deed,' as you put it."

He nodded. "You could be right."

"With that in mind," she went on, "I'd like to suggest a small, elegant affair—with our families and maybe a few of our very close friends in attendance."

"Sounds good to me."

"Maybe a candlelight ceremony?"

"I could warm to that idea."

"I'll wear a white dress, most likely silk, with a short veil—"

"Is that allowed?"

She punched him. "Jerk!"

He laughed as he dodged her attempt at a right cross. "You left yourself wide open for that one!"

"Yeah? Well, imagine yourself in a tux, sweetheart," she told him.

"No way!" He advanced on her menacingly. "There's no way on earth you're going to get me into one of those monkey suits."

"No?" she asked. "Would you care to put your money where your mouth is, *honey?*"

"Anytime, *sweetheart,*" he said, rising to her challenge.

"How much can you afford to lose?" she quipped.

"I was just about to ask you that very same question."

"Fifty?"

He laughed. "Not very sure of yourself, are you?" he asked.

"A hundred, then."

"I was thinking of something a little more interesting," he said with a sly smile.

"Like what?" Amy eyed him suspiciously.

"Oh, I don't know…"

"Don't play coy with me, Reynolds," she told him. "You've got something in mind—I can tell."

"Maybe."

"No maybe about it!"

He grinned. "I'll tell you about it on the way back to your mother's," he promised, breaking into a run, headed in the direction of his Jeep.

"Chicken!" Amy called after him.

"He hasn't come out of that room, even for a minute, since he went in—before the two of you left," Patti reported to Amy and Brian upon their return to the Barrington home.

Brian grinned. "Maybe they decided not to waste any more time than they already have," he suggested. "You know, go straight to the honeymoon."

Patti looked horrified. "I hope not!"

Amy laughed. "Now I know why Mom picked me to live with her after the surgery," she told her sister. "You're too overprotective."

"Don't be absurd!" Patti sniffed disdainfully. "She asked you because you're unattached."

"A status that's about to change rather dramatically," Brian interjected as he possessively slipped an arm around Amy's waist.

"An event that's restored my belief in miracles," Patti teased.

Brian turned to Amy. "Maybe we ought to reconsider this marriage business," he told her with what appeared to be genuine concern.

"Brian!"

He wrinkled his nose. "I'm not sure I can deal with having her for a sister-in-law," he confided.

Patti eyed him with mock indignation. "The feeling's mutual," she assured him.

Amy stepped between them. "I can see now that it's really a good thing that Brian and I are going to be living in Maine," she said.

Brian's gaze drifted to the top of the stairs. "What do you think they're doing up there?"

"Making wedding plans."

He looked at Amy. "Do you really think they've gotten that far?"

"Absolutely," she answered with certainty. "Your father doesn't have all your hang-ups about commitment."

"Hang-ups? What hang-ups?"

"How much time have you got?" she teased.

He still looked surprised. "You really think he's proposed already?"

"Already?" Amy asked, amused. "When we found him in that bus station in New Hampshire, he was on his way here to propose marriage to my mother."

"He told you that?"

Amy nodded.

"When?"

"This morning."

"Where was I?"

"Out in the rain—apparently trying to figure out why the Jeep wouldn't start," she told him.

He drew in a deep breath. "He really does love her, doesn't he?" The question was directed more at himself than at Amy.

"Yes," Amy said softly, touching his arm. "Do you still have a problem with that?"

He shook his head. "No. In spite of the problems

we've had in the past, I do love my father—and I do want him to be happy, for once in his life."

"But?" Amy had the distinct feeling there was more.

"But," he began with a heavy sigh, "there's a part of me that's always going to wish things had been wonderful between my parents, that they could have really loved each other."

She frowned. "I'm sorry."

He took her in his arms. "On the other hand—"

She looked up at him. "What?"

"If it hadn't been for his love for your mother and the ineptitude of the postal service, you and I would never have met," he said, kissing her forehead.

"If it hadn't been for the ineptitude of the postal service, we would never have been born!" she giggled.

"And I would never have known what I was missing."

She kissed him. "Maybe this would be a good time for us to finish our discussion," she said.

"What discussion?"

"About the tux."

He shook his head emphatically. "Oh, no," he told her. "No way. No way on earth am I going to—"

She kissed him again.

"No!"

Again.

"Well, maybe…"

Again.

"What the heck? It's only one night!" he surrendered.

She laughed. "Since you're being such a good sport about it, I'm not going to hold you to our bet," she said, tracing his lips with the tip of her index finger.

"Oh?" He was clearly enjoying this.

"No." She kissed him again. "I don't really want to wait, anyway. We've both waited too long already to start a family of our own."

Epilogue

"If anyone had told me—even six years ago—that I'd be getting married at all, let alone in a double ceremony with my own father, I would have said they were nuts."

Brian struggled with his tie until Jerry stepped forward to help him with it. They were in a small room at the church, dressing for the wedding.

"Funny. Katie said pretty much the same about you at breakfast this morning," Jerry chuckled as he checked his breast pocket to make sure he had the rings.

"The last thing I ever wanted to see was my father marrying the woman I spent most of my life hating because I held her responsible for the failure of my parents' marriage," Brian said then.

Jerry nodded. "You didn't exactly make a secret of that," he commented.

"Unfortunately."

"Unfortunately?"

"I've never seen my father as happy as he's been

since he and Marian found each other again," he said. "Katie was right all along."

"About?" Jerry stepped back as he finished with Brian's tie.

"She didn't believe Marian was the reason Mom and Dad broke up," Brian said, checking Jerry's handiwork in the full-length mirror on the dressing room door.

"Yes, she told me."

"She was right. She always said they just didn't belong together," he remembered. "I didn't even know what that meant until I saw Dad and Marian together. They belong together. There's something there, between the two of them, that was never there for him and Mom."

"As it is for you and Amy?" Jerry asked.

Brian nodded. "I suppose I had to experience love myself before I could recognize it," he decided.

"I guess," Jerry agreed.

John came into the room then. "Do I look okay?" he asked hesitantly.

Brian smiled. "You look fine, Dad," he assured him.

"You sure?"

"Have I ever lied to you?" Brian asked.

John made a face. "Come to think of it, no," he conceded. "There were times I wished you would—but, no, you didn't."

"Nervous, John?" Jerry asked, heading for the door.

"Nervous? After all these years?" John laughed. "Nah, just anxious to get on with it. At my age, every minute counts."

Jerry opened the door. "Shall we get on with it, then?" he suggested.

John nodded. "Can't happen soon enough for me," he said, following Jerry's lead.

"Brian?"

"I'm coming," Brian said, pausing just long enough to make sure he hadn't forgotten anything.

Nothing could go wrong today.

"You're worrying for nothing, Mom," Patti told Marian. "You look wonderful."

She stood behind her mother, who sat at the dressing table, fussing with her hair. Marian wore a pale blue suit that flattered her pale skin and dark, graying hair. Around her neck she wore a single strand of pearls.

When she was satisfied with her hair, Patti took Marian's hat from its hatbox. It matched her suit, a simple pillbox with a short veil. She positioned it on her mother's head and adjusted the veil. "All right?" Patti asked.

"I think so." Marian turned. "Amy?"

Amy stood in front of the only full-length mirror in the room, where Katie had been helping her dress.

She, too, wore a suit—ivory silk, with a short skirt and beaded lapels. Her hair was a mass of soft waves that framed her face, topped by a wide-brimmed, ivory silk picture hat.

"You look terrific, Mom," Amy assured her.

"You don't look like you, though," Patti said, giving Amy the once-over.

Amy raised an eyebrow. "You don't like the suit?"

"I love the suit," Patti said. "I've just never seen you wear anything so...elegant."

"In other words, you expected me to be married in denim and leather." Amy laughed.

"Well, no—"

"I'll bet you did," Amy chided, adjusting the brim of her hat.

"No, I didn't!" Patti insisted.

"They still squabble, just as they did when they were children," Marian told Katie. "That's the one thing about my girls that never seems to change."

"The same could be said of my brother and me," Katie responded.

"It's the law of nature," Patti decided.

Marian noticed that Amy had moved to the window and was not taking part in the conversation. "Patti, would you and Katie excuse us?" she requested. "I'd like a moment alone with Amy before the ceremony."

"Sure, Mom." Patti and Katie left the room.

After they were gone, Marian turned to look at Amy. "Are you nervous, my dear?" she asked.

Amy shook her head. "Just doing a reality check," she admitted.

"Reality check?"

Amy nodded, turning to face her. "A part of me never really believed this day would come," she said.

"Why not?"

"When I married Parker, I was so sure," she recalled. "I felt like I knew him as well as it was possible to know another human being—but look how that turned out."

Marian joined Amy by the window, taking her daughter's hands in hers. "We all make mistakes, my dear," she reminded her.

"I swore I'd never marry again," Amy remembered.

"Fortunately, you changed your mind—and here we are," Marian told her. "You know, when I thought John had stopped loving me, I told myself I'd never even look at another man again—but your father changed my mind, and we had forty wonderful years together."

Amy smiled. "You really did love Dad, didn't you?" she asked.

"I did, and with all my heart," Marian answered honestly.

"I'm glad."

"Now, we'd better go," Marian said. "You don't want to be late for your own wedding, do you?"

It was a beautiful ceremony: simple but elegant, straightforward yet full of tenderness and love. The two couples took their vows before a small group of family and close friends by candlelight, with a reception at Kirks' Bed and Breakfast afterward that was rowdy, upbeat and fun.

"You are going on a honeymoon, aren't you?" Katie asked Brian and Amy after they'd cut their wedding cake.

"Of course!" Amy laughed, dabbing icing and cake crumbs from her lips with a napkin.

"Where are you going?"

Brian smiled slyly. "I'll never tell," he insisted.

"You can tell me, big brother," she insisted. "I know how to keep a secret!"

"Right. It would be like telling the wire services."

"Brian!"

"What about those two?" Jerry asked, nodding toward Marian and John, who were cutting their cake at the moment.

Amy grinned. "You'll never guess," she said.

"Where are they going?"

"Atlantic City."

"Atlantic City?"

"You do know that was the in place for lovers when they were...well, young," Amy reminded him.

"Oh, yeah—the boardwalk and all that."

"Exactly."

"Have you two decided where you're going to live yet?" Patti asked.

"Right here in Burke's Harbor," Amy answered without hesitation.

"We'll most likely have to start house hunting as soon as we get back from our honeymoon, though," Brian put in. "I think the newlyweds are going to want to be alone." He nodded toward John and Marian.

"I'm hoping for a place near the water," Amy said. "What I'd really like is a place with enough rooms for me to have an office—one with a window facing the ocean."

"I'll be happy anywhere," said Brian.

"As long as we're together," Amy agreed.

"Absolutely," Brian said. "After all, how else can we start a family?"

They couldn't wait.

* * * * *

At last the wait is over...
In March
New York Times bestselling author

NORA ROBERTS

will bring us the latest from the Stanislaskis as
Natasha's now very grown-up stepdaughter,
Freddie, and Rachel's very sexy brother-in-law
Nick discover that love is worth waiting for in

WAITING FOR NICK

Silhouette Special Edition #1088

and in April
visit Natasha and Rachel again—or meet them
for the first time—in

The Stanislaski Sisters

containing TAMING NATASHA
and FALLING FOR RACHEL

Available wherever Silhouette books are sold.

NRSS

Bestselling Author

MARGOT DALTON

explores every parent's worst fear…the
disappearance of a child.

First Impression

Three-year-old Michael Panesivic has vanished.

A witness steps forward—and his story is chilling.
But is he a credible witness or a suspect?

Detective Jackie Kaminsky has three choices:
1) dismiss the man as a nutcase,
2) arrest him as the only suspect,
   or
3) believe him.

But with a little boy's life at stake, she can't afford to
make the wrong choice.

Available in April 1997 at your favorite retail outlet.

 MIRA The brightest star in women's fiction   MMDFI

IN CELEBRATION OF MOTHER'S DAY, JOIN
SILHOUETTE THIS MAY AS WE BRING YOU

a funny thing
HAPPENED ON THE WAY TO THE
Delivery Room

THESE THREE STORIES, CELEBRATING THE
LIGHTER SIDE OF MOTHERHOOD, ARE
WRITTEN BY YOUR FAVORITE AUTHORS:

KASEY MICHAELS
KATHLEEN EAGLE
EMILIE RICHARDS

When three couples make the trip to the delivery
room, they get more than their own bundles of
joy...they get the promise of love!

Available this May,
wherever Silhouette books are sold.

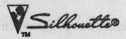